"A must read for everyone, young and old with adventures in their heart and a love for the great outdoors."

-Jack Lewis, Sourdough Mining Company Restaurant, Anchorage, Alaska

"Vivid, Panoramic, authentic: Glen Guy has captured the real Alaska for all ages. He has done a superb job in the tradition of Louis L'Amour and Zane Grey of capturing the sights and the sounds and the feel of the Last Frontier."

-Jim Rosen, Publisher, *Alaska People Magazine*

"Your stories give joy and pleasure to our elderly people. They ask to hear them every day. Every rest home should have your books and tapes."

-Heidi L. Angle, Heidi's Place, Palmer, Alaska

"If you like Louis L'Amour's Hondo, you'll love Dusty Sourdough."

-Larry Kaniut, author of *Alaska Bear Tales*

DUSTY SOURDOUGH
AND THE GREAT ALASKAN
ADVENTURE

DUSTY SOURDOUGH
AND THE GREAT ALASKAN
ADVENTURE

GLEN GUY

TATE PUBLISHING
AND ENTERPRISES, LLC

Published by Tate Publishing & Enterprises, LLC
127 E. Trade Center Terrace | Mustang, Oklahoma 73064 USA
1.888.361.9473 | www.tatepublishing.com

Tate Publishing is committed to excellence in the publishing industry. The company reflects the philosophy established by the founders, based on Psalm 68:11,
"The Lord gave the word and great was the company of those who published it."

Book design copyright © 2012 by Tate Publishing, LLC. All rights reserved.
Cover design by Rodrigo Adolfo
Interior design by Rodrigo Adolfo

Published in the United States of America

ISBN: 978-1-62147-140-0
FICTION / Action & Adventure
FICTION / Westerns
12.08.23

DEDICATION

To my loving wife, Sandy (Miss Aura Lee). Without her undying love and encouragement, Dusty Sourdough might never have come to life between these pages.

And a special thanks to the staff in the Alaska section of the Loussac Public Library, Anchorage, Alaska.

PROLOGUE

Just around the corner, about a century ago
There walked a transplanted cowboy named Dusty Sourdough
He came to the great north with mountains majesty
He came to Alaska to fulfill his destiny

The Old West was changing fast
And Dusty knew his way of life couldn't last
So, with mind made up and his things in his pack
He started north and would never look back

The many things he would soon gaze upon
From the mighty grizzly to the Sitka fawn
Oh the beauty and the wonders he will see
Along his northern journey to fulfill his destiny

Here in the vastness of this majestic land
Where everywhere you looked was the touch of God's hand
Here at last, he could truly be free
Living all of life's adventures on his road to destiny!

—Glen Guy

PART ONE

CHAPTER 1

Dusty, a cowboy turned mountain man, knew he was in trouble, even though he was a greenhorn or a "Cheechako," as the "Sourdoughs" called him, up here in this beautiful but dangerous land called Alaska.

The hours of daylight in the winter are few, and Dusty noticed that this day seemed shorter than usual. The dark, steel-gray sky to the north was getting darker by the moment, and his instincts told him that he had better find shelter and find it fast.

Up ahead, just beyond a crystal-clear but fast-moving stream, Dusty could make out a hollow in the rocky face above the stream bank. Now, you have to know, a stream to an Alaskan looks like a raging river to most Cheechakos, and Dusty wasn't any different than any other newcomer to this vast wilderness.

The closer he got to the stream, the more worried he became. His attention on the problem looming before him, in the fading, cold, gray light had him so bewildered that he didn't even notice the snow beginning to fall.

"If a man were to fall into that fast-moving, ice-cold water, odds of surviving isn't in his favor," he said to himself.

At about this time, Dusty finally noticed the snow coming down at an alarming rate. As a matter of fact, he could barely make out the rocky face of the stream bank, which was no more than a hundred yards away.

Desperately, he looked up and down the stream for anything, a dead fell, rocks, or even a narrowed place to jump across. He knew time was running out and if he didn't get across now, he would be a goner.

Just about the time he thought Mother Nature had dealt him a dead man's hand, he noticed, not more than twenty feet away, almost covered white with snow, an old birch tree leaning at an angle from the opposite bank out over the water. He knew if he could get a rope on it, he could swing to the other side, high and dry.

Now, you would think, being a cowboy and spending time working on a rancho near the pueblo Los Angeles, a little village down south, he wouldn't be worried about being able to get his lazo around a non-moving object like an old tree. Wrong!

For the first time, Dusty noticed how cold it had turned. His fingers were practically frozen as he tried to untie the knot holding his lazo to his pack. After three tries, he finally got it free and started for the stream bank, saying to himself, *Just don't slip and go into that icy stream, causen' no one will find your ole carcass 'til the snow melts in the spring.*

As he got set in a spot where he figured he could get a loop around that ole tree on the other side, Dusty looked up at the sky that now looked like one giant snowflake and mumbled something that sounded like this: "Lord, I know I'm an ornery ole cuss, and I ain't never asked you for much, but if you'll help me ta get this here lazo around that there tree, I'd be much obliged…and I'll try not to be so dang ornery too."

So with that said, he shook out a big loop, swung it around his head a couple of times, and let her fly. Now, to Dusty, it seemed like a lifetime before that loop settled over the top of that ole tree, but in less than a heartbeat, there she was, just as pretty as ya please, snugged tight right around that ole tree.

Chapter 2

Dusty tied off the lazo so it wouldn't end up on the other side without him and quickly put on his gear. Then he reached for the rope, and in the blinding snow, he got ready to swing across.

By now, the stream bank on the other side was nothing more than a shadow, and the hollow he had spotted just minutes ago was completely gone from sight, but he knew it was somewhere behind the solid white wall of falling snow. There was nothing left for Dusty to do except hope that he could find the hollow that was there only moments before.

With rope in hand and all the strength he had in his legs, he leaped for the other side with snow stinging his face in places where his beard didn't protect it. Not being able to see a thing, Dusty could only hope he had swung hard enough to reach the other side.

Just as these thoughts were going through his mind, there was a sharp report. It was so loud, at first, Dusty thought his old Hawkens 54 had went off by accident. No such luck! All of a sudden, he was falling, falling straight down toward the freezing water. In that instant, Dusty prepared himself for the big splash into the icy water that never came. Dusty and that rotten ole tree hit the bank with so much force that snow and rocks flew in every direction.

After realizing that he wasn't in the water like he thought he would be, Dusty quickly took inventory and found only his backside to be in any pain. He laughed and said to himself, *Boy, what a ride! Thank ye, Lord!*

Getting to his feet, he noticed that the snow wasn't letting up. Instead, it was coming down even more than before, so he knew he had to hurry. Starting up the bank in the direction where he thought the hollow should be, Dusty found the going next to impossible. The bank was almost shear rock and ice, with no real footing or handholds. Dusty's strength was being zapped by the intense cold and the climb up the bank that now looked never ending.

Pulling himself up on a small ledge no wider than his rifle stock, Dusty found himself looking into not just a hollow but a cave opening not much bigger than would permit his body to pass through. Cautiously, he crawled in the opening, and instantly, he could see nothing. Fumbling in his possible bag, he found a Lucifer and struck it on the rocky ceiling above his head. Without warning, he heard a blood-curdling roar, and felt a sharp pain start at his head and go all the way down his left side. A pool of blackness started coming over him. He tried to hang on, but he felt himself slipping away, and then nothing.

CHAPTER 3

Dusty didn't know where he was or how long he had been out, so he just lay in the dark on the hard packed ground trying to clear his head.

For the first time, Dusty smelled an odor that would turn the stomach of the strongest willed man, and if you had ever before got a nose full of it, you knew right then and there what it was. And with this realization, Dusty all but stopped breathing, trying to hear even the smallest sound. Nothing. Should he try to move? How bad was he hurt? Was his Hawkens within reach? And if so, how could he shoot what he couldn't see? Laying in the pitch black cave, Dusty knew that he had to do something. If he laid there, he would either freeze to death or be killed. He had no idea how far back the cave went or if the animal was even still in there with him, but he had to find out.

Very slowly, he reached out his left arm, and as he did so, a searing pain racked his body and he felt himself slipping away again. He couldn't let it happen. He had to hang on. And once again, the cocoon of unconsciousness took all the awareness of pain away.

Chapter 4

Dusty didn't know how long he had lain there, unconscious, this time. The sudden light caused him to jerk his hand over his eyes, causing the pain to hit him again, but this time, he didn't pass out. Slowly removing his hand and opening his eyes, he could see that he was still in the cave. But was it the same cave? Immediately, he noticed that the rank smell wasn't present. In its place, a pleasant aroma was coming from the back of the cave, where a fire was burning brightly and was the obvious source of light that had shocked his system just moments before.

Trying to stand brought waves of nausea and dizziness. For a fleeting second, he thought he was going down. Even managing to stay upon one knee was a feat in itself. The pain his body was going through no man should have to endure.

As Dusty tried to ease the burning, white-hot pain in his arm, he reached over and found that his left shoulder had the buckskin sleeve cut away and a bandage put in its place all the way down to the elbow. Further investigation found the same kind of bandage carefully placed around his head. Looking slowly

around, he said to himself, *What in tarnation is a-goin'
on? Where am I?* His gaze at that moment fell upon his
Hawkens, possible bag, and the rest of his equipment
that was stacked neatly a few feet from the fire. As his
eyes grew more accustomed to the firelight, he also saw
a large pile of firewood and a large iron kettle setting on
a flat rock next to the fire. This, he knew, was where the
pleasant smells were coming from.

With all the strength he could muster, he willed
himself to his feet. He stumbled and fell several times,
only shear willpower and the desire to keep living got
him to the fire and the food that was waiting there.

After eating directly out of the kettle with a wooden
spoon he found lying next to it, he felt like he just might
make it.

Lying back against a rock next to the fire, he began
to ponder, for the first time, how this all came about.
He remembered striking the match when he entered
the cave and smelling the obnoxious odor, then the
sudden excruciating pain, and then the nothingness.
As he was remembering the sequence of events, an
involuntary shudder shook his body, bringing him back
to the present. He looked about but could see very little
beyond the circle of firelight. Realizing he hadn't yet
retrieved his Hawkens, or even attempted to check
the rest of his gear, he started toward it. Knowing you
never leave your gun out of reach, Dusty knew that luck
had been kind to him this time. After checking what
he could, Dusty returned to the fire, and then an old
feeling crept into him, one he couldn't ignore.

CHAPTER 5

When he was younger and wandering around down by the Yellowstone, doin' a little scoutin' for the cavalry, this same feeling had come over him, a feeling that someone was watching him. Two days later, two Sioux jumped him and almost relieved him of his hair.

Looking into the darkness beyond the fire, this same feeling took hold of him. His eyes tried to see what only his imagination could. Where was he? And where did the fire, food, and stack of firewood come from, and what about the bandages? Was his benefactor out there in the darkness? Why had he saved him? These and many other questions were in Dusty's mind as he turned back to the fire. If whoever it was wanted to kill him, then why all this? It didn't make sense.

As the snow falling outside became a full-blown blizzard, Dusty tried his best to stay awake. The warm fire and his full belly was more though than he could contend with. His head nodded once, twice, and then sleep overtook him.

Chapter 6

Shivering from the bone-freezing cold that surrounded him, Dusty woke from a fitful sleep. It was pitch black and cold beyond belief. For a moment, he thought he had only dreamed the fire and the food. Reaching up, he touched his head and knew that it wasn't a dream. The bandage was still in place, and he could smell a faint odor of smoke left from the fire.

It was so dark that Dusty could only feel around for the makin's of a fire. Finding what he needed, he had to try several times to get a Lucifer to stay lit long enough to get a fire started. As the fire got going, he sat back to regain his strength.

Once again, Dusty could feel eyes watching him. Trying not to look obvious, he started a careful search with his eyes, first looking as far as he could to the left and then back to his right. Getting up as if to add more wood to the fire, Dusty caught, out of the corner of his eye, the glimpse of an object the size of a small bolder lying on the ground. Turning ever so slowly toward it, Dusty could see that it wasn't moving. Only then did he let out the breath he had unconsciously been holding. As Dusty approached the object on the floor, he couldn't believe his eyes. Sometime while he had slept, his benefactor had returned. Reaching down and touching the warm hunks of moose, he realized that it couldn't have been that long ago.

Dusty slowly turned around, saying, in a voice he tried to make sound confident, "Hey, pard. I sure do want ta thank ya fer patchin' me up and all this here grub! I'd sure enough like ta shake your hand. Why don't ya mosey over 'n sit a spell by the fire? It's yours anyway!"

Dusty didn't hear anything in return. Just the sound of the crackling fire and his own heart trying to beat its way out of his chest. The suspense was starting to get on Dusty's nerves. Moving back to the fire, Dusty decided he had enough and needed to find a way out and had to do it soon.

Getting the makin's and his coffee pot from his pack, he put some coffee on to boil. Taking his knife out, he sliced a good size hunk of meat from the haunch that was left him and put that over the fire to broil. Dusty turned from the fire and froze. Not more than ten steps away, a pair of mean, piercing eyes was looking at him. This in itself all but stopped his heart, but the low, rumbling snarl that came next turned his blood cold.

CHAPTER 7

For the second time, Dusty was out of reach of his Hawkens, and this time, it looked like his luck had run out. He tried to move, but again the vicious snarl came. Dusty felt little beads of sweat running down the side of his face, he knew that at any moment, this creature could spring for his throat, and all he had was a knife to defend himself.

Dusty, speaking in a low, gentle voice started talking. "Feller, ya don't want to eat ole Dusty. I'm as tough as buffalo hide. Why, I ain't had a bath since last spring. How's 'bout we make a deal? I'll give ya the rest of this here moose, and then ya go on your way." Slowly, Dusty backed toward the meat that was still lying on the floor. Picking it up, he said, "Here ya go. Come and get it."

As Dusty moved closer, to his surprise, instead of the vicious snarl, a low whimper came from the piercing eyes that now didn't seem so menacing. Holding the meat out and continuing to talk softly, Dusty moved closer. Ever so slowly, the outline of an animal took form, first a head, and then the rest of the body.

Dusty laid the meat down and slowly retreated. As he moved back, a big, white wolf-dog cautiously stepped into the firelight. The animal, with an eye on Dusty, picked up the meat and disappeared into the darkness.

At first, Dusty didn't move. Listening, he could hear the animal eagerly tearing meat from the bone. He hoped it would be enough to curb his appetite.

Moving to the fire, Dusty removed his meat, waited for a brief moment, and then started eating. When he was finished, he threw the remains into the darkness, where the wolf-dog had retreated.

Dusty was never been one to kill an animal just for the sake of killing. From the time he was a little boy in Tennessee, he loved to watch the wildlife that abounded around his folk's farm, and he tried to make friends with all of them.

Now with this great, white wolf-dog sharing his sanctuary, he had to make a decision. Should he try to kill him or try to make friends with him? While pondering this question, the decision was suddenly taken out of his hands. The dog had silently slipped up to within arm's length, laid down by the fire, and was fast asleep. Dusty sat for the longest time just staring at the pure, white creature. The longer he sat there, the more he realized that he couldn't kill it. Something in his heart told him this wolf-dog was not going to harm him.

With that thought in mind, Dusty said to the sleeping dog, "You sure enough had me goin'. When you first growled, I thought you wasin' that big ole bar a-comin' back ta finish me off. Shucks! Ya weren't even a little bar. Ya were just a hungry ole dog a-huntin' a hand-out. Well, if ya mind your manners, we can pard up 'til we get out of this here fix."

The wolf-dog, hearing Dusty talking to her, raised her big head and whimpered softly as if to say, "Okay," and then settled her head back down between her front paws and was fast asleep.

Chapter 8

Dusty didn't know how long he had been asleep. The cave was almost dark, except for the red glow coming from the dying coals of his fire. What had aroused him from his sleep, he didn't know. And then, out of the darkness, a few steps to his left, a low but very deep growl came. In an instant, the wolf-dog was on her feet and charging off into the darkness.

Ever so slowly, Dusty stood up and, with his Hawkens in hand, moved to the fire. After he got it roaring again, he picked up a small limb he could use as a torch and moved in the direction the wolf-dog had taken. He could hear or see nothing, so venturing farther into the darkness, he came to an abrupt end and was facing a solid rock wall.

Dusty couldn't believe it. "Why, I knowed that wolf-dog came this a-way," he said to himself. Looking down, he could see wolf tracks leading right up to the wall and then stopping. "Wait a minute," Dusty said. "These here tracks lead up to this here wall, but none led away. It's as if that wolf kept a-goin' right on through that there rock wall."

Dusty stood there in bewilderment, not believing what his eyes were telling him. Holding the torch close to the ground, Dusty started back-tracking the wolf. As he approached the campfire, he looked up. Much to his disbelief, there, laying by the fire, was the great white wolf-dog.

Dumbfounded and not realizing what he was doing, Dusty walked up to the big animal and reached down to pet her. At that instant, he froze. What in the world was he doing? This animal could tear him apart. "Well, girl, I guess now's as good a time as any to answer two questions I got in my mind I need a-answerin'. First of all, are you real, not a shadow or a spirit? And secondly, can we be pards?"

Carefully, Dusty squatted down before the wolf-dog and slowly reached forward to stroke her head. To Dusty's surprise, this animal only licked at him and seemed to enjoy the human touch. "Well now," Dusty said, "you sure enough are real, and I can tell you're a-likin' your ears scratched. I guess I'll just have ta give you a name and trust you'll side me if the goin' gets tough."

If only this great, white wolf-dog could talk, she would tell Dusty how she drove the grizzly out of the cave and then stood guard until she was lured out by a strange noise she couldn't identify. If she had known an ancient Indian wolf call had been used so a man could enter the cave and tend to Dusty, things might have turned out different. By the time she had searched the areas beyond the cave, the stranger had managed to come and go without being seen, leaving behind a roaring fire, a patched-up Dusty, and a kettle of stew cooking on the flames.

When she had returned to the cave, the new smells made her cautious, and being part wolf, she didn't completely trust man, so when Dusty started stirring, she moved off into the shadows to see what this human would do.

Dusty, looking down at this beautiful, white animal, which was obviously part wolf, couldn't understand how she had come to be here and, even more curious, why she had befriended him.

"Well, girl," Dusty said, "we have to find a name befittin' a great heart like yours. Let's see. Your being here has certainly lifted my spirits, and when I first saw you in the shadows, I thought you might be a ghost or a spirit of my imagination." Dusty threw another log on the fire and as he watched the sparks dance upward, a knowing smile came across his face. "Why, that's it. That's what I'll call you, Shadow Spirit. How's that, girl? You like that? Shadow Spirit." As Dusty said the name over again, her tail began to wag as if to say that she approved.

The blizzard had blown itself out the night before, so Dusty knew he had to try for the little gold rush town of Hope. Another storm could come along at any time, and Dusty didn't want to take the chance of being trapped in the cave permanently.

The rest of the day was spent making ready to leave the cave. Dusty, still in pain from his wounds, moved about slowly, resting often. When this occurred, Shadow Spirit would come to him, and the two would spend these moments getting to know each other. By the end of the day, all was ready for an early morning departure, and a bond between Shadow Spirit and Dusty had been formed that would last a lifetime.

CHAPTER 9

Dusty woke early the next morning, even though he wasn't going to leave until some indication of light appeared in the sky. After rustling up some breakfast, he crawled through the small opening to have a look at the day. He decided it wasn't going to get any better. He was surprised to find the morning still in semi darkness, the clouds hanging low with a threat of more snow in the near future. He decided if he was going to leave, he'd better light a shuck, he was burning daylight—or what would pass for daylight.

The sky was still a leaden gray, and the temperature was well below zero when Dusty, with his pack on his back, Hawkens in hand, and his new companion at his side, headed into the unknown wilderness and toward a place called Hope.

Dusty knew that it would be slow going, but just how slow, he had no way of knowing, and every step took a monumental effort. In places, the drifts were so deep that Dusty would have to find another way around, sometimes taking an hour just to move ahead a few feet. At times, a great wind would blow down from the mountain peaks, picking up snow, causing what was called a white-out. Dusty tried to keep moving during these periods, but he became very disoriented and, in no time at all, was hopelessly lost.

About this time, when desperation was starting to undermine Dusty's thoughts, he noticed Shadow Spirit acting peculiar. She would run off a little way in one direction and then return whimpering and pawing at him as if to tell him to follow her.

When it finally dawned on Dusty what she was doing, he jumped to his feet, praising Shadow Spirit, saying, "Girl, I should have known you'd know the way. After all, you already saved ole Dusty's life once, so why not trust you with it again."

As if she understood every word Dusty had spoken, Shadow Spirit let out a loud bark and headed down the direction she had been trying to show him.

The snow was just as deep as before, but Shadow Spirit seemed to know the easiest way to travel, for in no time, she had led them back to the trail Dusty had wandered from.

CHAPTER 10

Dusty and Shadow Spirit had been on the move most of the day and, by now, were in deep woods. The big evergreens and spruce had protected the forest floor from the past blizzard, and the snow that had penetrated their lush, green boughs was minimal. The trail was well marked, and Dusty decided to call a halt for the day. It didn't take long to set up camp next to a small stream and get a warm fire going.

Dusty, thinking ahead as he got ready to leave the cave earlier that day, had packed the last of the moose meat his unknown benefactor had mysteriously left him. Now, as the thoughts of his benefactor played on his mind, he couldn't help but cast a worried look into the deep, dark woods that loomed just beyond the light of his fire. Was whoever it was lurking in the shadows? And if so, what was he waiting for, or why?

As Dusty broiled his moose meat and entertained these thoughts, Shadow Spirit sprung to her feet and charged into the dark forest with a growl. In an instant, even before Shadow Spirit's growl had died away, Dusty had his Hawkens in hand and had, himself, disappeared into the safety of the dark forest.

The sky, if Dusty could have seen it, was a glow with a billion stars and alive with the dance of the Northern Lights. Even though this was going on above him, at this point in time, he wasn't concerned with the beauty of the night, even though as a kid, he loved watching the stars move across the velvet-black skies of a Tennessee night. On his mind at this moment, he was trying to figure a way out of this situation. Already, he could feel his joints stiffening up from the bitter cold.

From directly behind him, something or somebody was crashing through the underbrush, coming straight for him. With his adrenalin pumping and his reflexes taking over, Dusty sprang to his feet, whirled around, and brought his Hawkens to his shoulder, waiting for a clear shot. Just as sudden as the noise had begun, it stopped. Dusty didn't know what to make of it. He unconsciously took a couple of steps back and froze. Something was behind him. He slowly turned around and faced the camp. There, lying by the fire, as if nothing had happened, was Shadow Spirit. As he approached her, her tail began to wag and a happy whimper came from deep within.

Dusty couldn't sleep, so he sat with his back to the fire—this way, his night vision wouldn't be affected—and pondered the mysterious actions of Shadow Spirit, remembering how she seemingly disappeared through a solid rock wall and reappeared a short time later, just like tonight, lying by the fire like nothing had happened. The more he thought about it, the more uneasy he felt. He knew in his heart there wasn't an answer, at least not one that made sense.

Dusty had no idea what time it was or how long he had sat there. The fire had burned down some, and all the familiar night sounds had returned to the forest.

CHAPTER 11

Throwing a few more branches on the fire so he could boil himself some coffee, he made ready to continue his trek to Hope.

It was still dark when Shadow Spirit and Dusty started down the mountain trail. When daylight finally started showing itself, Dusty figured it to be at least ten or eleven in the morning, and he knew darkness would be returning in less than six hours. The trees had thinned some, and he could see the sky, which, by now, was once again a threatening gray, and a light snow was beginning to fall. Stopping for a brief rest by a big, ole fallen spruce, Shadow Spirit came and sat by Dusty's side.

"Well, girl, if you could talk, maybe you could tell me how much farther we have to go. I was in hopes we could make town by tonight, in case this weather turns into something we'd want no part of."

He reached down and patted her head. His love and admiration for this beautiful white wolf-dog had grown so immense that he couldn't imagine walking the forests and trails without her by his side.

Now looking down at her, he could see urgency in her face that wasn't there before. Without warning, she sprang to her feet and shot off down the trail, looking back once to make sure Dusty was following behind, and then she disappeared out of sight.

As the day wore on, the snow continued to fall at a slow rate, making it hard at times to climb over rocks that had fallen on the trail sometime in the long-ago past. After climbing over such an area, Dusty stopped to get his breath and saw Shadow Spirit bounding toward him, her excitement visible even from a distance. As soon as she reached his side, she was off again, headed over the ridge, barking wildly as she went. Dusty couldn't imagine what was so exciting on the other side and couldn't wait to crest it and see for himself. The surprise he looked down upon as he struggled over the top thrilled him beyond words. Below him stood a body of water, bluish gray in color and very cold looking. Looking to the left just a little, he could see what Shadow Spirit was so excited about. Right next to the water's edge was a small settlement. A few of the log cabins already had their lanterns lit, for darkness was fast approaching.

Shadow Spirit was nowhere to be seen as Dusty walked down the street, if you could call it that. It was very narrow, not much wider than a path. One of the biggest buildings on the right had a sign on it that read "General Store," so that's where he headed. As his foot hit the first step, he heard a bark behind him and turned to see Shadow Spirit running toward him with a man running close behind.

The man approached Dusty and said, "Excuse me. I see you have already met my dog, Snow. My name's Patrick, Patrick Reilly. My friends call me One-Eyed Reilly."

Dusty didn't know what to say. He just stood in the middle of this little town with his heart breaking, realizing that Shadow Spirit wasn't his but belonged to One-Eyed Reilly. He reached out and shook hands with him and said, "Glad to meet ya. That sure is one fine dog ya got there." Trying to put on a smile that wouldn't betray his sadness, he followed Shadow Spirit's master into the store, which served as a central meeting place for the town.

One-Eyed Reilly introduced him to George Roll, the owner, and poured them a cup of strong, black coffee that was being kept warm on the big stove in the center of the store. Dusty told them of his narrow escape from the grizzly and how Shadow Spirit—Snow—had saved his life. And then he told of the food and the mysterious fire that was left in the cave. He even told of the strange feelings he had that someone was watching him. When he had finished, he thought One-Eyed Reilly and George would break out laughing, but instead, they looked at each other with a knowing expression on their faces, and a long silence followed.

At last, George spoke, and his voice was so low that Dusty had to strain to hear what he had to say. "Well," he started, "between here and Chickaloon Bay, there's a point of land that the Athabaskan Indians had themselves a burial ground on. Some of the white men hereabouts went up there and raided their graves for the possessions that were buried with them. The Indians say that because of this, the spirit of one of the Indians buried there walks the trails leading over the mountains, looking for men with evil in their hearts. I'd say, Dusty, you had a run-in with that there ghost, unless you have a better answer. I sure don't."

The silence was thick in the store when One-Eyed Reilly finally spoke. "That's some story, George. It's the kind to tell kids around a campfire to scare 'em."

They all laughed, but you could tell that it was a nervous laugh.

Looking at Dusty, One-Eyed Reilly asked, "Ya need a place ta stay? I got an extra bunk over at my place. It ain't much, but it's warm."

"Thanks! That sounds real nice."

So they said their good-byes, and then Dusty followed his new friend toward his cabin and a good night's rest.

The cabin was a typical miner's dwelling. It had one room with two bunks in the corner, an all-purpose stove at one end, a table with a lantern sitting in the middle, and a couple handmade chairs. The usual pots and cooking tools hung on the wall next to the stove, and a pile of firewood was stacked nearby.

Closing the heavy plank door, One-Eyed Reilly said, "I told ya it weren't much. You can have the bunk on the right. I kinda favor the other one myself. We'd better turn in. Tomorrow's Christmas Eve, and we have a little shindig over at the store. It's a time when the entire town turns out for some of Mrs. Roll's hot cider, and other ladies bring their best recipes. Believe me, it's a time your stomach ain't wantin' to miss, and it's also the time when we exchange gifts with each other. See ya in the morn." And with that, the ole miner turned the lantern out, crawled into his bunk, and was asleep before his head hit the pillow.

Dusty couldn't fall asleep. His thoughts were of Shadow Spirit, and of how he was missing her already, even though she had come and laid on the floor beside his bunk. His hand reached down and touched her soft, white fur. She gave a big sigh and went back to sleep.

Looking down at her, he knew that he didn't want to go to the get-together. He didn't have a gift to give, and his heart wouldn't be in it. With these and other thoughts running through his mind, Dusty finally closed his eyes and fell into a fitful sleep.

CHAPTER 12

Dusty woke to the smell of bacon frying, something his nose hadn't smelled in a good, long while. Shadow Spirit was still lying by his bunk and came to her feet when Dusty rolled out.

"Good morning, girl. Did ya sleep well?"

The dog put her front paws in the middle of his chest. This was, he was sure, her way of returning his greeting. Affectionately, Dusty rubbed her ears and gave her a loving pat.

"That ole dog sure has taken to ya," the miner said. "She doesn't come around much, except to eat and get warm. I don't even rightly know where she came from. She just showed up one day and decided to stay. Well, breakfast is ready. Hope ya like bacon and sourdough pancakes."

Setting down to a huge stack of flapjacks and more bacon than he could possibly eat, Dusty said, "I reckon I can get around these vittles," and with a big smile on his face, he went to work on the best breakfast he'd had in a mighty long time.

The day dragged slowly for Dusty. By the time it rolled around to head for the get-together, he had resigned himself to going, even though his heart wasn't in it.

As he and his newfound friend walked through the door, the smells of Christmas hit him full in the face. At first, no one noticed the two of them standing there. That is, until Shadow Spirit let out a joyful bark announcing their arrival. All heads turned to look for a brief moment and then returned to their conversations. Dusty, relieved to see this, turned away from the crowd and looked for a place to sit. Finding a bench that was close to the stove, Dusty sat down and waited for the night to end.

As the evening wore on and it came time to exchange gifts, everyone started to gather around the stove. Dusty didn't know what to do. He had chosen to sit by the stove because everyone else was at the other end of the store. Now, to his chagrin, the whole town had gathered around him. Dusty stood up to move away from the crowd and was stopped in his tracks by a voice that sounded like the whisper of an angel. Turning to his left to see where the voice was coming from, he couldn't believe his eyes. Standing not more than a foot away was the most beautiful woman he had ever seen. Not only did her voice sound like an angel's whisper, she even looked like an angel. Her hair was the color of corn silk, and her eyes were as blue as a summer sky. And when she smiled at him, he got goose bumps all over. Dusty didn't know what to say. His lips were moving, but nothing was coming out. Finally, he managed a, "Howdy, ma'am, I…I'm Dusty Sourdough, and I think you're 'bout as pretty as a new speckled pup." *Boy, was that a dumb thing to say,* he thought to himself.

"Why, Dusty, that's about the nicest thing anybody has ever said to me. I'm pleased to meet a man who can speak his mind. My name is Aura Lee."

Dusty knew as he was looking into her eyes that this was the lady he wanted to marry. "Excuse me," she said. "I have to exchange gifts with my friend now. I hope we will see each other again so we can talk some more." With that said, Aura Lee turned and walked away.

Dusty was completely befuddled when One-Eyed Reilly came up to him and said, "I see you met Aura Lee. She's the only single girl in town. You're not married, are you?"

"No," Dusty said, "but I sure would like to be."

"Yeah, and I bet I know who ya got in mind," the ole miner said with a twinkle in his eye.

"Well, all the gift exchanging has been done except for mine."

One-Eyed Reilly said, changing the subject, "I wasn't givin' a gift ta anyone. I didn't think I had anything ta give, but I was wrong. This morning, when I saw the bond between you and Sn…I mean Shadow Spirit, I knew you two were meant for each other. My new friend, please accept her as a gift from me, and Merry Christmas."

Dusty didn't know what to say. He reached down and gave Shadow Spirit a pat and said, "Merry Christmas, girl. You're the greatest gift anyone has ever given to me."

"Don't go gettin' all choked up. It's only a dog. It's just a dog."

Chapter 13

By the time Dusty, One-Eyed Reilly, and Shadow Spirit returned to the cabin, it was well past midnight.

While the old miner was banking the fire for the night, he asked Dusty about his plans and if he was going to stay long.

Dusty thought about his new friend's questions, and when the answers came to him, he realized that the driving force behind them had to do with only one thing or, as he said to himself, one person. "Well, I'll tell ya, up 'til tonight, I was plannin' on leaving tomorrow, but I have ta be truthful! I think I fell in love tonight. If I was ta leave now, before I tried my best ta get Aura Lee ta marry me, why, the rest of my life, I'd be a-wonderin' about her and if she would've had me. So I reckon I'll stay around a while and see this ta the end."

With a sleepy voice, One-Eyed Reilly said, "I knew you weren't going anywhere the minute I saw that puppy dog look on your face after meetin' Aura Lee. If ya like, you're welcome ta stay here as long as you need."

"Thanks, ole friend. Ya make me feel right welcome. Makin' friends like you along life's road to destiny sure enough takes some of the bumps out of that rough ole road. I know my adventures up here in this beautiful land have just begun. Who knows who I might run into on this trail I've chosen? Shucks, I might even be a part of history! Only time will tell."

PART TWO

CHAPTER 14

Even though almost everyone in town was saying this winter was the worst they could ever remember, Dusty couldn't have been happier. Of all his adventures as a cowboy, cavalry scout, and Indian fighter on the Western frontier, nothing ever had seemed to hold his interest. He was always looking for what was waiting on the other side of the hill and when arriving, whatever he was looking for wasn't to be found, so another hill awaited him and his never-ending search. Dusty didn't know at the time, but his journey north would be the end of his lifelong quest. In this land, he would at last find peace and his trail to destiny in a settlement called Hope on the last frontier.

The town meeting was well underway when Dusty and Shadow Spirit stepped through the door. "As we all know," George Roll was saying, "this winter is a bad one, one we hope only comes along once in a lifetime. I know all of ya is runnin' short on grub, and I have ta tell ya the store is too. As ya can see fer yourselves, the shelves are practically empty. Johnny Dynamite hasn't been able to get the *Utopia* up the inlet to re-supply us, and no one has made it over the pass since Dusty did, back before Christmas."

Just the mention of that narrow escape from the cave up on Resurrection Pass gave Dusty a very uneasy feeling. It was the same feeling he had back in the cave, when the hair on the back of his neck would stand up, warning him that a pair of unseen eyes were lurking somewhere in the blackness of his sanctuary. Sometimes when he and Shadow Spirit ventured into the nearby forest to get familiar with the surroundings, that same feeling would come over him. Something or someone was watching him.

Dusty's attention was brought back to the meeting by the sound of V.O. Rollie's voice saying, "I reckon if I don't get me some meat and dry goods, I'll have ta be a-closin' my grub tent. One of us is gonna have ta go a-huntin', and I mean right soon. There won't be help a-comin' from Fort Resurrection. With all the snow we've had, there's no way a body could get through the pass. So who's it gonna be? Who's a-volunteerin'?"

With that question, the room became dead quiet. It was so quiet you could hear the crackling fire in the old pot belly stove and the steady ticking of the Regulator clock hanging on the wall above the empty dry goods barrels. After what seemed like an eternity, Dusty heard his own voice saying, "Why, shucks, I reckon I could give it a try. While I was down in the Wyomin' territory a few years ago, I worked for the railroad a-huntin' buffalo ta feed the crew that was a buildin' what I called the end of a way of life."

As Dusty spoke, no one noticed the sadness that came into his eyes. The life that he once knew as a cowboy and a free spirit in the Old West, he knew, would never come again. With the railroad and the invention of barbed wire, the West was changing fast and the open range would soon be no more.

Then, by chance, on a wet, gray, rainy day in a Seattle waterfront cafe, Dusty met a man named King who would change his life forever. As King told his story of gold just lying on the ground for the taking in a place he called Alaska, Dusty thought his ore cart was a few shovels short of a full load. That is, until he pulled out four pokes of gold. This got Dusty's undivided attention. The more King talked about this place he kept calling "the last frontier," without a shadow of a doubt, Dusty knew destiny was calling him to this vast wilderness of the midnight sun, a place called Alaska.

"Oh, Dusty," Aura Lee cried, jumping to her feet with fear in her voice, "why should you be the one to go?" Aura Lee then turned to face the surprised town folks and asked, "What's the matter with all of you? How can any of you let Dusty go into the bush? He hasn't been here long enough to know how to survive a blizzard or a sudden drop in temperature. Someone else just has to go! Please, please don't let him go!"

Again, there was nothing but silence. No one would look her in the eyes. Not a person spoke up to volunteer.

Finally, in an even, steady voice, Aura Lee said, "You're all a bunch of cowards, and if you let Dusty go, and if something happens to him, I'll never forgive any of you!" With that said, she spun around in a flurry and stomped out of the store. Everyone looked at each other in astonishment, or should I say amazement. Until now, they all thought Miss Aura Lee was a quiet, meek schoolteacher. Now they knew better.

"Now, would you ever in your born days imagine that sweet little lady havin' grit like that?" the storekeeper asked.

Everyone chuckled, breaking the uneasy feeling permeating the store.

The code of the West carried up to the last frontier, and part of that code was not to ask a person about his or her past, so when V.O. Rollie cleared his throat and began to speak of his past, it piqued everyone's curiosity.

"I guess before Dusty came to town, I was the Cheechako around here. I know ya all have often wondered why I don't wear a gun." The next words that came from the normally jolly café owner was a surprise to everyone. "First of all, I wasn't always a cook and cafe owner. Before I came to Hope, I was a lawman for fifteen years in the Arizona Territory. I was a good one too. That is, until the day the McKinney gang came to town.

"The westbound stage had just pulled up in front of the Wells Fargo office. All of a sudden, the peaceful morning stillness was shattered by the unmistakable sound of gunfire. When this all started, I was at the barber shop, getting a shave. I sprang to my feet; wiped the shaving soap from my face; and out the door I went, colt in hand. A bullet smashed into the door jamb above my head. Throwing myself to the ground, I fired back at one of the gang members who was running for his horse. That's when it happened.

"It felt as if I had been kicked in the head by a forty-dollar army mule, and then a searing wave of pain racked my entire body. I closed my eyes and clenched my teeth, trying to make the pain go away. When I opened them, everything started moving in slow motion. I tried to lift my colt, but my arm wouldn't respond. The gun went off, firing into the dirt.

"After that, I didn't know a thing until I came to, in bed, at Millie's boarding house with Doc Barns a-standin' over me. He had a real worried look on his face, and when I tried to speak, I couldn't make anything come out. I must have passed out again, because the next time I regained consciousness, Millie was by my bedside, and the look of concern on her face wasn't any more encouraging than that of Doc Barns.

"I said I was thirsty and asked for a drink of water. You could see the relief flow into her face. As we talked, she filled me in on what had happened.

"The McKinney gang was robbing the Wells Fargo office of the gold shipment that had arrived on the westbound stage. She said that I had tried to stop them, but they had me outnumbered ten to one. Lead was flyin' around like a bunch of mad hornets. I was shootin' back and holdin' my own too. I even plugged me one of those pole cats, but that's when I almost went under. I got hit in the head, just above my ear, by a ricochet. Doc Barns said I had the hardest head he had ever seen."

Removing his hat, V.O. lifted his hair above his left ear and revealed a ghastly two-inch scar. "It took me months before I was able to get around on my own, and at last, I thought I was pert near healed. I was fixin' ta go back ta sheriffin' when Doc Barns came by my room and told me something that would change my life forever. He said the dizzy spells that came over me at unsuspectin' times would probably always happen. In fact, he said they could get worse and I should consider another line of work. If I should have a dizzy spell or even pass out with my colt in hand, it could go off and shoot an innocent bystander. It would be tough to live with if that ever happened. After three days of thinkin' on it, I turned in my badge and hung up my guns forever.

"After that, I just drifted for the next two years. What happened in that time wasn't important. To make a long story short, somehow, I ended up here in Hope, slinging hash in my grub tent. I truly wish I could be the one to go huntin', but I'm sad to say I don't even own a gun any longer."

As Dusty sat there, listening to V.O. lay his past bare for everyone to judge, he couldn't help wondering about all the other untold stories in the room. It took some nerve to do what V.O. had done, and Dusty couldn't help admiring him.

The rest of the men came up with their own reasons for not being able to leave town. Some, like Charlie Miller, were afraid of claim jumpers taking over their mines if they were gone too long. Others had pretty feeble reasons, and Dusty couldn't help wondering about their mettle.

"Well, I reckon I best go clean and oil my ole Hawkens and get my gear ready. I'll be a-leavin' at first light in the mornin'. That is, if no one else has an objection."

With Shadow Spirit by his side, Dusty walked out the door and into the cold, crisp Alaskan night.

Chapter 15

Aura Lee, stumbling from the store with tears flowing freely down her cheeks, was making her way back to her quarters, located in the rear of the schoolhouse. She knew she had made a fool of herself. Now the whole town knew of her feelings for Dusty.

Oh well, she said to herself. *I hope Dusty doesn't think I'm too outspoken and won't want anything to do with me.*

As Aura Lee turned down the path leading to the schoolhouse, a noise coming from behind her caused her heart to skip a beat. Whirling around with a fear-constricted throat and a shaky voice, she managed a, "Who…who's there? I've a gun… I-I know how to use it!" She stammered, looking into the darkness. Standing as still as a statue, she could hear her own pulse beating like a drum, but to her relief, she could hear nothing else.

With weak knees, Aura Lee turned and started down the path. She hadn't traveled but a few steps when she heard the noise again. As she started to turn, a crashing sound came from the dark forest. It was too late for her to do anything but brace herself for the inevitable attack.

CHAPTER 16

Dusty, with Shadow Spirit by his side, left the meeting at the general store and started for One-Eyed Reilly's cabin. The temperature was well below zero, and the night sky was like none anywhere in the world. Dusty stood in awe looking up at the spectacular show of the greens, golds, and other colors of the Northern Lights as they danced across the black, velvet sky of the Alaska night.

"It's a mighty cold night, ole girl," Dusty said, turning to pat Shadow Spirit on the head. But to his surprise, she was nowhere in sight. "Now where has that four-legged, tail-waggin' critter got to? She can disappear faster than anything I ever knowed. Shadow Spirit! Shadow, where in tarnation are ya?" Dusty called and called, but to no avail. There wasn't even an answering bark, only the whisper of the wind in the snow-laden boughs of the surrounding forest.

"If she doesn't show up by mornin', I guess I'll just have ta leave without her." With that said, Dusty turned and continued down the path to the cabin. As he reached the door, he glanced up his back trail, pulled the latch, and went inside. Dusty took down his old caliber 54 Hawkens, cleaned and oiled it, and then got his trail-worn pack out from under his bunk.

Aura Lee was right. Dusty didn't know much about surviving in this vast wilderness. A man could freeze to death in moments if he didn't know how to stay warm, and that wasn't the worst thing that could happen to him. With as much care as possible, Dusty started putting jerked moose, flint and steal, fire starter, dry socks, and the rest of his trail gear into his pack.

Reaching for the shelf above the stove for coffee makin's, his hand froze in midair. Were his ears playing a trick on him? Did he hear a scream, or was it just the wind? Dusty strained to listen for the sound he thought he had heard only moments before. There! There it was again!

He wasn't imagining it. Pulling on his heavy fur coat and with his Hawkens in hand, he charged out the door and down the trail toward the sound that had interrupted his packing.

⌒

Fear struck, Aura Lee spun around. As she did so, her foot slipped on the snow-covered trail, and she fell down onto her backside with a thud. Before she could recover her footing, the menace from out of the dark forest was on top of her. At that same moment, as a big, pink tongue came across her face, she recognized her assailant and burst into laughter with relief and joy.

"Shadow Spirit, you scared the wits out of me. You should be ashamed of yourself," Aura Lee said as she stood, brushing the snow off and then reaching to give the big wolf-dog a loving pat on the head.

"Hey!" a voice called from the dark. "There ya are, ya old scallywag," Dusty exclaimed. "I guess ya decided to go a-callin' without me. Ya should be ashamed of yourself, botherin' Miss Aura Lee that-a-way."

"Oh, she's no bother, Dusty. She just gave me a fright for a moment."

"Well, if ya'd like, me un her'd be glad ta walk ya the rest of the way home." Dusty volunteered with shyness in his voice that he hoped she didn't notice.

"Why, that would be right nice, and maybe you would like to come in and sit a spell…I mean have a cup of tea…I mean coffee…I mean…" Aura Lee could feel the red flush of embarrassment traveling up her neck and into her face. The harder she tried to be nonchalant, the worse it got.

Dusty, chuckling to himself, saw the predicament Aura Lee was working herself into, and interrupted her by asking, "Have ya got any of that there sugar stuff? That would go right nice in a cup of coffee."

While Miss Aura Lee got a fire going in her cook stove and prepared the coffee, Dusty couldn't help but notice how comfortable her quarters were, and it was then, while looking about, that an unfamiliar feeling came over him.

In all his days, he never thought he could be so content sitting in a parlor, but to his surprise, he was, and more than that, he found himself not wanting it to end. It was hard for Dusty to say good night after enjoying a sweet, hot cup of coffee, not to mention the warmth he felt in his heart when in the company of Aura Lee. He knew he had to finish getting ready for his adventure that would start at first light in the morning, so Dusty reluctantly said his good-bye and headed for the door.

"Wait!" Aura Lee said, reaching for a brightly colored woolen scarf hanging on a hook by the door. "This will remind you that you have a home-cooked meal with dried apple pie for desert to come back to."

"Golly, Miss Aura Lee. Are ya a givin' me an invite ta dinner when I get back from huntin'?"

"I…I guess I am. Please be careful, and don't take any chances you don't have to."

Starting back down the trail with thoughts of Aura Lee dancing in his head, Dusty didn't hear Shadow Spirit's first warning growl. When the second one came, it was much more intense, and this time, it got Dusty's undivided attention. Another low growl came from deep within her chest as he turned in the direction the wolf-dog was looking.

Dusty brought the hammer back on his Hawkens and stood stock still. The forest was dark and ominous, and when Dusty called out, there wasn't an answer forthcoming. It was then that Dusty noticed something very strange. Shadow Spirit was still growling and even barking toward the forest, but now her tail was wagging.

"Hey, girl. What's going on here? Are ya givin' me a warnin', or are ya greeting an unseen friend?" Puzzled, Dusty reached down and stroked Shadow Spirit's head. It was then that he noticed that the hair was standing up on the back of his neck. "There's someone out there watching us, girl, but I don't have ta tell you that, do I? Come on. Whoever it is, I don't think he's going to show himself. He seems ta just want ta watch us fer the time bein'. We've got more to do before we can light shuck in the morning."

After getting the rest of his things together for the hunt, Dusty lay down on his bunk and quickly fell off to sleep.

⁓

Dusty didn't know what had awakened him or even how long he had been asleep, but he knew that something or someone had awakened him, and whatever or whoever it was, the hair on the back of his neck was standing up.

Lying there in the dark, ears straining for the slightest sound, Dusty remained motionless. But for what? What had awaked him?

Sensing Shadow Spirit's movement more than seeing it in the darkness, Dusty reached down beside his bunk and felt that the big wolf-dog was alerted and stock still, with her ears pointed toward the door.

"What is it, girl? Do ya hear somethin' out there?"

With a bark, she sprang for the door. Dusty leaped to his feet and grabbed his trousers with one hand and his Hawkens with the other.

"Hold on, hold on. Let me get my pants on."

As he reached the door, the whole inside of the cabin lit up with bright lantern light. "Hey, what's all the ruckus? Can't a feller get some shut-eye around here?" One-Eyed Reilly said as he blew out the match.

Before One-Eye could utter another word, Dusty was out the door, following Shadow Spirit. Pausing at the edge of the clearing surrounding the cabin, he stopped to figure out which way Shadow Spirit had gone. He couldn't hear a thing; not even a bark or a growl came from the dark forest to indicate the direction she had gone. Standing in the sub-zero temperature for a moment, it didn't take Dusty long to decide to return to the warmth of the cabin and let her chase whatever it was that had awakened them.

One-Eye was up and getting the cook stove fire going when Dusty stepped through the door. "Well?" he asked with a puzzled look.

Dusty explained how he had been awakened and could see or hear nothing when he went outside to investigate. One-Eye just shook his head when Dusty had finished and offered no explanation to the strange goings-on, but as Dusty talked, a strange look came over One-Eye and what appeared to be a nervous tick started twitching at the corner of his mouth.

CHAPTER 17

After a huge breakfast of sourdough flapjacks, birch syrup, bacon, and plenty of hot coffee, Dusty got his gear on, said his good-bye, and stepped into the early morning light. He headed through town and picked up a trail that went west along the inlet toward Chickaloon bay.

He hadn't gone far when the familiar sound of Shadow Spirit's bark came to his ears. Turning, he saw her charging up his back trail as fast as her legs could carry her. When she reached him, he bent down and stroked her big head, saying, "Hey! What's the rush? I knew you'd catch up ta me sooner or later. Where ya been? I sure wish ya could talk. I bet the conversation would be right interestin'."

Unfortunately, all she could do was show her happiness by her body movements and that forever wagging tail.

"Let's get on down the trail and see about huntin' up some meat!"

The trail was well marked and easy to follow, so Dusty and Shadow Spirit were making good time. The inlet waters shimmered like liquid gold in the breaking light of a jeweled morning as the sun broke over the snow-covered mountains to the east. Breakup was underway, and it wouldn't be long before the ice would be gone from the valleys. Even now, Dusty could feel the warmth of sun on the side of his face as he came to the edge of a clearing. There were a heap of tracks in the clearing, and by their size and shape, Dusty knew a moose had passed this way, and it hadn't been too long ago.

Speaking to Shadow Spirit in a hushed tone, Dusty said, "It looks like we're in luck. These here tracks are fresh, so we'll need to move real careful like. Ya understand?"

He was always amazed how well she understood his every word. As he started tracking the moose across the clearing, Shadow Spirit, close on his heels, fell in behind at full alert. The trail led up and away from the inlet and into the trees. At first, the going wasn't bad, but after a short distance, the climb got steeper and Dusty found himself stopping more frequently to rest. It was during one of these rest periods he noticed the sun had given way to some very menacing gray clouds.

The wind had picked up and carried with it a message that Mother Nature wasn't ready to give up her icy grip on winter, not yet. More than once, Dusty had heard people say how unpredictable the weather was up here in this far North land, and now he was about to find out just how harsh the sudden changes could be.

It wasn't long before the snow started falling lightly. It always astounded Dusty how still and beautiful it became during a gentle snowfall, and he was hoping that a gentle snowfall was all it was going to be.

The moose tracks were getting more arduous to follow, and the snow was coming down harder when

Dusty caught a glimpse of something moving through the trees up ahead. Dropping to one knee and bringing his Hawkens up, he waited, hoping that at last, he had caught up to the moose he had been tracking for most of the day. In that moment of thought, out it stepped, the biggest moose he had ever seen.

When it stepped into the middle of the trail, Dusty's reflexes must have taken over because he couldn't even remember pulling back the hammer on his Hawkens. All he heard was the thunderous roar of it going off and then the huge animal going down. Dusty reloaded his rifle and then, with the utmost caution, slowly approached the animal that would put meat on the dinner tables of Hope. The moose was huge. Close up, it looked as big as or bigger than any animal Dusty had ever taken for food.

"Well, Lord, I sure do thank ya for this magnificent creature," Dusty said as he got ready to dress and skin it. "I reckon ya know how much I dislike destroyin' any of your critters, but I promise I'll use every usable part." With that said, Dusty got to work.

After skinning and quartering the moose, he then addressed the problem of getting it back to town. He knew he wouldn't be able to take it all with him, so he decided to cache the bigger share of it high up in one of the nearby spruce trees. After fulfilling this task to his satisfaction, he and Shadow Spirit had a cold lunch of squaw candy and hard tack, and then they started back down the trail to Hope.

As darkness settled over the vast untamed wilderness, Dusty was disappointed at the amount of trail he had struggled over in the short amount of daylight that was allotted him on this cold winter's day in Alaska. In the past four hours of gray, cold light, he was sure the distance wasn't more than a mile, and probably closer to a half mile.

The wind had come up and, at times, blew ice crystals in Dusty's face that felt like thousands of needles hitting his leathery skin. This, in itself, Dusty had grown used to since he had come to the North Country. What was really ticking him off was the fact he wasn't going to make it back to his cabin by suppertime, and that meant that he would have to eat his own fixin's one more night. Well, that's not really the whole truth either. Since the Christmas party at the general store a month or so ago, ole Dusty had been doin' a heap of sparkin' with Aura Lee. Every time his thoughts would turn to her, and that was more often than he would admit, his ole heart would go to beating like an Indian war drum and his mind turned to mush.

Just before Dusty had left to hunt up fresh meat for the town, she had promised him she would come over and fix him a home-cooked meal that would knock his hat in the creek.

As total darkness surrounded him and his great wolf-dog, Dusty went about getting a fire going and coffee boiling. "Well, ole girl," he said to her as he worked, "if this here wind hadn't come up, we sure enough would've tried to make the cabin even in the dark."

Shadow was lying by the now-warm fire, looking at Dusty with her ears forward, as if she knew every word he was saying.

Over the past months, the bond between Dusty and Shadow Spirit had grown so strong, that when you saw one, the other was always close at hand. Most of the time, if you asked Dusty about the obvious affection between them, he'd say. "Ah she's just an ole wolf-dog taken to followin' me aroun'." But everyone knew different. I'd sure pity the person who tried to lay a hand on that ole wolf-dog.

There was gentleness about Dusty, and he had an uncanny way with animals, but at the same time, you knew if he had to be, he could be as tough as a grizzly and twice as ornery. When Dusty had warmed himself with a strong, steaming cup of coffee, he noticed that the stars were becoming visible and the wind had died down to a gentle breeze.

"Well, Shadow, ole girl, maybe we stopped too soon. The moon ought ta be up in a couple of hours, and it's goin' ta be full. What say we pack up and hit the trail?"

In one bounding leap, Shadow was right smack dab in the middle of him, all excited and raring to go.

"I take it by all this commotion; you're ready to hit the trail right now."

With that said, Dusty systematically started packing up and, in just a few short minutes, was ready to light shuck. The trail was barely visible as they started out, but Dusty only had one thing, or should I say one person, on his mind. If he would have known what lay ahead of him this night, I'm sure he would have had second thoughts about starting out before the moon came up. Shadow was breaking trail as best she could, but the wind that had been blowing earlier that day had drifted the snow in places to where it was impossible to pass.

Finally, Dusty called her back to him, saying, "Maybe ya better let me do the trail breaking for a while. Them ole drifts are givin' ya a heap of trouble."

Dusty's admiration for his great white wolf-dog grew with each giant snow drift he had to fight his way through. When an open area appeared before him, Dusty was more than ready to take a breather. Ahead, he saw a log jutting out of the snow and decided to set his tired bones on it to take a much-needed rest. As he reached it, Shadow, a short ways behind him, started to bark and raise cane as if her tail was caught in a bear trap.

Dusty stopped in his tracks and spun around to see what the commotion was all about. In that instant, he knew that Shadow's warning had come too late.

CHAPTER 18

Snow started falling shortly after Dusty and Shadow Spirit hit the trail. One-Eyed Reilly had a bad feeling about it right from the start and decided to go talk to George Roll.

Trudging through the rapidly deepening snow, he reached the general store the same time as V.O. and several of the other concerned town folks. As usual, the store was cozy and warm, with the smell of fresh coffee. Unfortunately, this spur-of-the-moment gathering wasn't one of a social nature. On the contrary, it was one of concern. No one had even called it; they just came to the store because somehow they knew the others would be there. As in the past, whenever there was trouble, this was the place to come.

"This storm is turnin' into a mean one," George was saying as One-Eye was shaking the snow off his parka. "Dusty could be in real trouble, and we—"

At that moment, the door flung open, and Aura Lee rushed in. "I told all of you something might happen, and now look. It's a blizzard out there, and Dusty is caught in it!"

The room fell silent. Some of the men started fidgeting around looking in every direction except hers, others tried to look her in the eye but couldn't.

When One-Eye started speaking, it surprised everyone in the room. Generally, he was a man of few words and only spoke up when he had something important to say, so it went without saying that he had everyone's undivided attention.

"As I see it," he said, "one of us needs to be a-doin', instead of jawin'! I knew all of ya would be down here, so I just come down ta tell ya all I'm a fixin' ta hitch up my dogs and go fetch him back here. Don't no one try to change my mind, 'cause I'm a-goin'!"

Before anyone could react to One-Eye's short and to-the-point statement, he was out the door.

Back at his cabin, One-Eye hurriedly threw together what he would need to survive while searching for Dusty and then went outside to hitch up his dog team. With this done, he was ready to leave. With all but his eyes bundled up, he gave the command to mush and headed north along the trail toward Chickaloon Bay.

It was mid-morning when trouble struck. With One-Eye's vision limited by his patch, he didn't see the tree across the trail until it was too late to stop his team from getting tangled in the branches. The abrupt stop had thrown him headlong into a snow drift. This would have been hilarious if he wasn't on such an urgent mission, but time was of the essence, and this delay could be very costly.

His dogs were veterans and knew not to fight the entanglement. In a short time, One-Eye had them untangled and the sled righted, but then the hard part started. The huge tree had the entire trail blocked, and there was no visible way around. The only thing to do was get the ole ax out and try to chop his way through it. After three hours of nonstop chopping, One-Eye realized he needed help. The tree was too big to cut through with an ax. When he had come to this conclusion, he decided to start for town. The dogs had rested while he worked on the tree and were ready and willing to head back.

Knowing that darkness was fast approaching and danger lurked around every bend in the trail, One-Eye kept a grueling pace. As darkness finally swathed the land, the wind had died to a gentle murmur, and the snowfall was almost nonexistent.

"Well, if luck holds," One-Eye said, talking to himself, "I reckon we should hit town afore the moon comes up."

Looking into the night sky, One-Eye could clearly see patches where the clouds were giving way to the twinkle of stars shining like diamonds on a black velvet cloth. Less than an hour went by before One-Eye topped the last ridge and could see the lights of town below. In a matter of minutes, he was bringing his team to a stop in front of the store.

Someone had seen him coming, and the people inside were charging headlong through the door in excited anticipation only to be disappointed when they discovered that One-Eye hadn't found Dusty. After telling of the tree blocking the trail and how he tried to get through it to no avail, the tone in One-Eye's voice changed. When he spoke next, it was with a gentle plea to his voice that no one had ever heard before.

"I reckon all of ya know what I'm fixin' ta ask, and I surely wouldn't be a-askin' if I could've got through that there tree by myself, but…but I need help. I need someone to help me cut a trail through that there tree."

The silence that fell in the room was electrified with tension—with guilt. Whatever it was, it was broken when V.O.'s voice brought everyone back to the task at hand.

"You can count on me," he said. "It's time someone around here found some grit. Miss Aura Lee was right; we should have never let Dusty go. He could be seriously hurt or, God forbid, dead. One-Eye, I'll have my team hitched in twenty minutes. I'm sure Charlie will let you use his dogs. Yours have to be worn plumb out. We can get a block and tackle at the Smithy's' and I'll bring my whip saw. Why, we'll be through that tree like a hot knife through butter."

Turning to Miss Aura Lee, One-Eye said, "You just rest easy. We'll be back in no time with Dusty safe and sound." Even though One-Eye was exhausted, he moved with utmost speed and was ready to leave when V.O. was. The sleds were loaded with provisions and tools, and the moon was on the rise as One-Eye and V.O. headed north toward Chickaloon Bay.

In the distance, they could hear the plaintive call of a lone wolf.

Chapter 19

The ground violently pitched Dusty about like a rag doll. He grabbed for the log he had been standing close to, but it too was being tossed about. At that instant, a cracking, grinding sound came to his ears, and a cavernous crack opened at his feet. Looking down, Dusty could see cold, murky water and realized that the place he had chosen to rest wasn't a clearing at all; it was a small lake.

Looking about, after the ground stopped shaking, Dusty could see the power and destruction of an earthquake and wondered if there was more to come. The crack in the ice was a formidable barrier, and as he assessed his situation, what he found made it worse, much worse. To his dismay, he discovered that the crack encircled him completely. As Dusty mulled this over, his small, unstable island shuttered violently, knocking him to his knees. At that moment, he didn't have time to think; he only had time to react. Springing to his feet, in one smooth motion, he leaped for the other side of the cavernous crack that was even wider now than before. Dusty knew in that moment that he had made a grievous mistake. He wasn't going to make it! Reaching with all his strength, he grabbed for the edge of the crevasse as he hurled by it, heading for the icy, cold splash and the inevitable freezing death that awaited him in the murky water below.

To his surprise though, Dusty felt his hands hit the ice with a body-jarring smack, and then the scramble was on. His purchase was minimal at best, and he knew that his life depended on his own strength to pull him over the edge of the ice crevasse.

Dusty wasn't a big man; he stood only five foot six inches tall, but he was broad across the shoulders and had a barrel chest and arms as strong as a grizzly bear. Hopefully this strength would be enough to save him from a freezing, watery grave. With all the might he could muster, he began to pull himself, inch by inch, over the edge. Somewhere in the distance, Dusty could hear the frantic bark of Shadow Spirit, and for a moment, he wondered what she was barking at. His struggle and the cold was taking its toll. He could feel his arms weakening. Trying to get a better hold on the ice, he started to slip. Terror struck his heart and so many things came flashing through his mind at that moment. He didn't see the powerful hand reach down and clutch his wrist with a viselike grip. The next thing he knew, he was being pulled to safety by a giant of a man.

The Indian looked down at Dusty with what he conceived to be a hostile look, and in that brief moment, the thought crossed his mind that he was saved from a freezing death only to die a tortured one at the hands of this menace standing over him.

In the next instant, all fear left Dusty as a warm, gentle smile spread across this huge Indian's face. His eyes showed concern when he asked in perfect English, "Are you hurt, my friend? When the earth moved, as it often does here along the great water I feared you were lost and all that I had done for you, that my spirit had told me to do in the past, had been for naught. If your faithful companion and my longtime friend, the one I call Strong Heart and you call Shadow Spirit, hadn't led me to you, I am sure your life would have ended this day."

Dusty didn't know what to say. He was flabbergasted. *How did this stranger know I called my wolf-dog, Shadow Spirit? And what does he mean by, "all the things he's done for me in the past?"*

"Say, how is it ya know Shadow Spirit's name?" Dusty started to question." How is it that I ain't ever seen ya around afore? Who are ya?"

The Indian held up a big hand, putting a stop to Dusty's questions. "I will tell you answers to all your many questions, but we must leave here before the ground shakes again and we are trapped here on the ice. My camp isn't far; you can warm yourself by my fire and have some hot coffee. There, I will give you answers to all your questions and more."

The hike to the Indian's camp was short. It amazed Dusty how short. He considered himself an alert woodsman, and how he had missed the trail leading off the main one he had earlier traversed was beyond his comprehension.

The camp, located in a small clearing next to a small stream, was neat and looked inviting. Without the Indian, the fire had burned low. The coffee, sitting next to the coals, was still hot, and Dusty gratefully accepted a steaming tin cup of it.

As he was collecting his thoughts and forming the questions he needed answers to, the Indian began speaking.

"Many winters ago, I was banished from my village for being a friend to a Tlingit. They are our enemies from the south, and to befriend one is unforgivable. He had been attacked by the great bear, just as you had been, and needed my help. I took him to the same cave I took you to and stayed with him for several suns—I mean days. He had been mauled badly, and I could not help him much. He died one morning while I was hunting food.

"While trying to save this Tlingit's life, I was being spied on by an evil man from our village. When I returned, I was taken before the tribal council and banished from my people for life."

As Dusty listened, many things became clear to him for the first time. "Since ya saved me from that grizz—"

"No!" the Athabascan said. "I did not save you. Great Heart, I mean Shadow Spirit, did. She ran that bear off and then kept watch over you. I only brought you to my cave and took care of you until you regained your strength."

"Why did ya not show yourself?" Dusty asked.

"I did not know if you were friend or enemy, so I decided it would be best to stay out of sight and continue to help you from afar. After you recovered, there was no need for me to reveal myself, but my heart was worried that I might have helped an evil man that I should have let die. I have been watching you ever since. When you volunteered, at your town meeting, to hunt food for your village, I was outside the window. I knew then that I had done the right thing. You have a good heart, Dusty Sourdough!"

Dusty and his new friend talked a while longer. Shadow Spirit made herself comfortable by the fire, and in no time, she was sound asleep, as if nothing out of the ordinary had ever happened. Dusty too became sleepy and dozed by the warm fire.

Something hitting the ground next to him jolted him awake.

"Easy," came the voice of the Indian. "It is only I. While you dozed, I returned to the frozen lake and retrieved your gear. When light comes in the morning, you will have everything you need to continue your journey. Rest now. Morning will soon come."

After several hours of sleep, Dusty woke to the sound of familiar voices coming from down the trail. He couldn't believe his eyes when the sleds came into sight, carrying his two friends. "Well, I'll be!" Dusty exclaimed. "If ya ain't a sight fer sore eyes, I don't know what is. Boy! When that shaker hit yesterday, I thought I was a goner. If it weren't fer my Indian friend here." Dusty stopped in mid-sentence. Looking about, he discovered that the Indian was gone.

"What Indian?" V.O. questioned. "There isn't anyone here but us. Maybe you dreamed it! Sometimes your mind can play tricks on ya out here."

"No! I didn't imagine this. He was here, and he saved my life!"

"What's this feller look like?" One-Eye asked.

As Dusty described the Indian, his friends got a puzzled look on their faces. The description matched no one they knew or had ever seen.

"Does this friend of yours have a name?" asked V.O.

This question stopped Dusty cold. In their conversation around the fire the night before, he had neglected to ask that very question.

"I…I don't know his name. He never told me. But he was here. I know I wasn't imagining him. He was here!"

"Well, whether or not he's real, we can talk about it back in the warmth of George's store. Right now, I think we should hit the trail," One-Eye said with finality in his voice.

Before they started back, Dusty told of his successful hunt. After returning to his cache and loading the moose meat on the two sleds, they headed down their back trail toward home.

The return trip was uneventful. With the dog teams pulling the load, it was much faster than the trip out. The conversation was minimal, and the subject of the Indian never came up. As they topped the final ridge and town was in sight, something made Dusty turn and look back. To his surprise, standing at the edge of the forest was his Indian friend. There wasn't any doubt in his mind now that he was real, and Dusty knew that they would meet again.

CHAPTER 20

It was like a Fourth of July celebration in the spring. Everyone in town was in a festive mood.

Just knowing that Dusty was back and unhurt was enough to lift the town's spirit, but when they found out the hunt was successful, the people exploded with joy.

Everyone decided that the occasion called for a get-together, a potluck, and a dance at the general store. But unlike the last one, Dusty didn't need his arm twisted this time to attend. He was all for it. The shindig was set for the following night, and Dusty knew that Miss Aura Lee would be there. Anyway, he hoped she would be.

Upon his return, the whole town had gathered about him, everyone, that is, except Miss Aura Lee. When he looked about, he caught a glimpse of her through the crowd. She had tears in her eyes, and when she saw him looking at her, she turned and ran away.

Dusty didn't understand her actions. They certainly put a damper on his enthusiasm. She was the most important one he wanted to see. After the task of dividing the meat among the town, Dusty headed for One-Eye's cabin and a well-deserved night of rest.

The sun was high in the cloudless, azure-blue sky when Dusty woke from his restful sleep. "Well, it's about time ya rolled out!" One-Eyed Reilly said with a humorous chuckle. "I got the makin's all mixed up fer some of them there sourdough flapjacks ya favor. I reckon I ought ta call them Dusty's Sourdough flapjacks. Shucks, if everybody outside would take a likin' to 'em like you, I wouldn't hav ta work my fingers ta the bone a lookin' for gold anymore.

"Durned if ya don't come up with some rip snortin' ides," Dusty good-naturedly retorted. "One of these days, I do believe you're gonna come up with a new-fangled idea that will put some gold in your poke."

They both had a good laugh over this thought. Shadow Spirit even got into the act with a few joyous barks.

The day went by quickly, and before they knew it, the sky to the west was aglow with the setting sun. *Such beauty,* Dusty thought as he watched the sky change from a golden orange to a fiery red. "All this and still my heart has an empty place in it," he said to his ever-faithful companion, Shadow Spirit. "Well, girl, maybe I'll figure it out someday. I fer sure need somethin' in my life, I just can't imagine what it could be."

Almost everyone in town was at the store when Dusty and One-Eye walked in. The smells were tantalizing, and the jubilance in the air was overpowering. The children were playing hide and seek behind the dry goods while the ladies finished laying out their finest recipes. The men had gathered around the old, potbellied stove, listening to V.O. Rollie tell how he and One-Eye found Dusty.

As soon as they spotted him, cheers went up, and Dusty became the center of attention. Dusty didn't really like all the fuss bein' raised about him. By nature, he was shy and kept to himself. He felt as if everyone was staring at him, and he didn't know what to say.

"Good evening!" a voice came from behind him.

Recognizing the voice, Dusty spun around with a smile on his face as well as one of relief to see Miss Aura Lee coming toward him. She was absolutely the most beautiful lady he had ever seen. Her smile lit up the whole room and gave Dusty a warm feeling all over.

"Good evenin', ma'am. You're bout as purtty as the sun risin' on a spring mornin'!" Dusty said as he turned red with embarrassment. "I was affeered ya weren't gonna come tanight."

"Well…well I got something in my eye and had to go home. I'm sorry if you thought I was mad about something."

When Aura Lee finished speaking, Dusty saw something in her eyes. *Perhaps a plea?* He wasn't sure. Whatever it was, he chalked it up to his not being able to figure out women. When everyone had their fill of all the wonderful food, a fiddle and mouth harp appeared, and the music began. Throughout the evening, Dusty and Aura Lee were inseparable. It left no doubt in anyone's mind that love was in bloom.

If Dusty wasn't careful, he would be the first guy to get hitched in a place called Hope.

Chapter 21

As spring came to Hope, love came to Dusty in the form of Miss Aura Lee. They spent all their spare time together. When school let out in the afternoons, they would wander off with Shadow Spirit by their side and a picnic basket swung from Dusty's arm. The days were growing longer, and Dusty felt a peace within himself that had never been there before. His life was tranquil, and the beauty of Alaska in the spring was visible in every direction, but that was about to change.

One afternoon, as Dusty came down the trail leading to the school, the bell hanging outside began to ring with all the gusto a young feller could muster, knowing it meant school was out for another day.

"Good afternoon, young feller!" Dusty said with a smile. "It looks ta me like you're mighty happy school is out fer another day! Why, shucks! Back when I wasn't any bigger than you, my grandpa would have ta warm the seat of my britches pert near every week 'cause I'd play hooky and go fishin' instead of a doin' my book learnin'. I surely do wish I woulda listened to him. A feller needs ta do figurin and know how ta read and write in this here world."

Dusty looked down at this lad and smiled. He had a special place in his heart for the little ones, and somehow, they knew it. At times, all the kids in town would gather around him and listen in awe while he told his stories of the Wild West. Dusty had taken a special likin' to this little guy, who, by coincidence, like Dusty, was being raised without a father. Dusty didn't know the whole story, but he did know that he had left to go huntin' and never came back.

The wilderness is beautiful but generally unforgiving. A wrong decision or a misplaced step could mean disaster. In this case, it left this freckle-faced boy and his mother without a father and a husband to support them and to teach the boy things only a father could do.

"You'd better get on home and get to your chores. There ought ta be a heap o' light left when ya get done ta go fishin'."

"Yes, sir!" the young feller said and was off like a shot down the trail.

Shadow Spirit loved to play with the kids, and the feeling was mutual. She could spend hours romping through the spring grass with them, so when the kids came out, Dusty paid little attention as she went running off to play. Dusty knew she would catch up with them if she wanted to come along.

Dusty turned in time to see Aura Lee come out of the school with a smile on her face and a bounce to her step. As usual, just like the first time he laid eyes on her, his heart started beating like an Indian war drum. "Howdy! I just came by ta see if you'd like to go have a look at a little somethin' I been a-doin'. It's not too fer from here, and ya might be a-likin' it!"

"I have test papers to grade, Dusty, but if it won't take long…"

That's all Dusty needed to hear. Taking her by the hand, he headed down a trail toward a meadow they had picnicked at once. Dusty knew Aura Lee really loved this place with a crystal-clear stream running through it and tall fir trees all about.

When they were close to the meadow, Dusty stopped and blindfolded Aura Lee, telling her that what he had to show her was a surprise, and boy was it. In a matter of minutes, Dusty and Aura Lee stepped into a clearing.

Dusty, removing the covering from her eyes, said, "Well, what do ya think?"

Aura Lee stood staring, speechless, not believing her eyes. Before her loomed a beautiful cabin in the finishing stages of being built. The first thing she noticed was the covered porch. It stretched the entire front of the cabin, and when sitting on it, you could see a small creek sparkling in the sun, babbling by about two hundred feet away.

"Do ya like it? Come on inside. I-I built as best as I could remember," Dusty stammered.

"Remember what?" Aura Lee asked, and then it hit her like a sack of grain.

From the moment the blindfold was removed, something had looked familiar about the cabin. It was like the one she had always dreamed of. How could this be? She'd only spoke of her dream once in passing while at a town picnic with Dusty. "Oh, it's beautiful, Dusty! It's just like the one I have dreamed of so many times!"

Standing in the main room, she could see the big, spacious kitchen with a brand-new wood cook stove up against the right side. Next to it was a long, pine counter with shelves above and below. The front wall had a large window that enjoyed the same view as the porch. Under the window was another counter, and farther down the wall was a huge pantry with four cedar doors. Dusty had built a plank table, and it was sitting close to the window. The main room was spacious and airy too. The ceiling was open beamed with hand carved and fitted logs. At the far end was a beautiful fireplace made of river rock, which had taken weeks to select and carry up for the building of it. Halfway down the left wall, a stairway led to the second floor and what was to be the bedrooms. There were two of them. One was larger with a wardrobe closet and the frame of a partially built bed in it. The other room was much smaller and bare of any furnishing.

The smell of the fresh-cut logs and the afternoon sun streaming through the open windows made it all the more beautiful. To Dusty, the finishing touch was standing next to him, looking around at his labor of love, for he had built it for her and her alone.

"I sure do hope ya like it, causein' I have somethin' else I been a-meanin' ta ask ya. I mean, I've been a-wonderin'…I mean, do ya think…aha shucks! A purtty lady like you would never think of a-marryin' an ole, crusty, good-fer-nothin' like me. I ain't—"

Dusty didn't have time to finish.

Aura Lee threw her arms around his neck, saying, "Yes! Yes, Dusty! Yes! Oh, Dusty, you're not a crusty good-for-nothing. I've loved you since that first, 'Howdy, ma'am!' I was beginning to think you would never ask me. Come on. Let's get back to town so I can tell everyone and start making plans for our wedding! Dusty, you have made me the happiest girl in the whole world."

Dusty too was happy beyond belief. Stepping over the threshold with Aura Lee in hand, Dusty had failed to notice a subtle change in the surrounding forest. Any other time, he would have picked up on it immediately. The sounds of the forest were nonexistent. It was as if all the birds and critters were hiding in fear for their lives. If Dusty would have noticed this, maybe the next thing that happened could have been avoided.

A blood-curdling roar came from the side of the cabin. In one easy motion, Dusty turned to face his tormentor and, at the same time, grabbed Aura Lee and shoved her toward the door of the cabin. Then it charged. Pulling his Colt, he fired at almost point-blank range at the biggest, meanest grizzly he had ever had the misfortune of meeting up with. The shot hit the bear dead center, but it kept coming. The shot hadn't slowed him one step.

Dusty stepped backward just as the bear took a swipe at him with his lethal front paw. The razor sharp claws caught Dusty a glancing blow to his shoulder and knocked him to the ground. With catlike speed, Dusty rolled to the side and sprang to his feet. This seemed to confuse the grizz for a moment, and that moment was all Dusty needed to get his knife out.

The grizzly let out another death-defying roar and charged. This time, Dusty didn't back up. Instead, he lunged straight for the bear, ducking a massive paw that was aimed for his head. Now he was in the grasp of this huge carnivore and could feel and smell his hot breath on the back of his neck. Dusty pulled in as close as he could to avoid the gaping jaws of this man-killer and, at the same time, plunged his knife into the bear's rib cage.

The animal let out an ear-shattering roar, but this time, it was different. This time, it was one of pain. Still, the bear's grip was hugging the life out of him. Dusty became lightheaded from lack of air, and he knew that time was running out. He had to hit a vital spot with his knife if he had any hopes to survive.

The bear again was trying to get at Dusty with his powerful jaws. Looking up, he could only see fur and more fur. That was it though, and Dusty knew it.

When the bear's ugly yellow teeth were just inches from his face, Dusty stabbed his knife upward, into the mass of fur, where he thought his throat might be. To his surprise, the bear gave out a roar and released his death hold on Dusty. As he slipped free, the grizz started falling forward, and Dusty knew he could never get out of the way. He had lost too much blood, and his strength had slipped away.

The last thing he remembered, before the smothering weight of the bear crushed the consciousness from him, was a familiar voice he recognized, and it wasn't Aura Lee's.

Chapter 22

Slowly, Dusty became aware of voices and then light. Opening his eyes, he found himself looking into the face of his mysterious Indian friend.

"Lay still, my friend, while I finish bandaging these wounds," said the Indian. "That old rogue grizz didn't do as much damage as the last time, but that doesn't mean he didn't get in a few good licks. Lucky you were out cold. That way, it was easy for Miss Aura Lee to hold you down while I used this porcupine quill and sinew to sew up your shoulder. That ole grizz laid it open clean to the bone!"

"I guess it coulda been worse," Dusty said. "He coulda taken my head off!"

"I reckon he was still mad at you for waking him up early last winter before he got all his beauty sleep."

"How do ya figure he's the same one that was in the cave?" Dusty asked his Indian friend.

"Two reasons," he said. "One, that grizz in the cave had only three toes on his right, front paw, like the one you just killed. The second reason is this piece of arrow I dug out of his neck. I put it there myself when he was on the run from that cave.

"He was one mean bear, and I doubt that you were his first human victim. You were just the one that got away. Speaking of getting away, I never in my born day seen anything like it, the way you wrestled that grizz, I mean. In my village you would be honored and looked upon as having great powers. When what you have done becomes known, there will be no one that doesn't know the name of Dusty Sourdough, the one who slays grizzlies with his bare hands!"

"Well thanks, but I was just tryin' ta keep my hide in one piece. Speakin' of names, what handle do ya go by? It seems ta me that I oughter know the feller's name who's pulled my bacon out of the fire three different times!"

"My Indian name, in your language, means, 'One That Walks Alone.' I was given that name when I was banished from my village."

"I reckon it's 'bout time you get a new one then, 'cause as long as ole Dusty is a-kickin', you won't be a-needin' a handle like that. No friend of mine ever has ta walk alone. I'll just shorten it some. How 'bout Walker? If'n yar needin' it longer, how's Walker, Dusty's friend!"

"After…Walker and I skin and butcher that brute," Aura Lee said, "do you think you have the strength to make it back to town?"

"Why, sure!" Dusty said with a little indignation in his voice. "I'll even skin that ornery critter myself. I feel fine! I've gotten hurt worse tryin' ta shave. That's why I got this beard!"

Even though skinning and dressing a grizz is a tall order, it didn't take as long as it would have with only one person doing it. Aura Lee surprised Dusty when she rolled up her sleeves and started butchering as fast as the men skinned the hide back. By dark, they had the job done and stored the meat in a cache that Dusty had built behind the cabin. The meat would have to be salted, smoked, and preserved as soon as possible, but for now, this would have to do.

❧

By late afternoon the trio finally made it to the General Store and most of the town folks had gathered and were introduced to Dusty's mysterious Indian friend, who told the story of the bear attack on Dusty. They stood in amazement that Dusty had escaped with his life and only a few claw marks on his shoulder to show any sign of a violent attack. After a few more questions, Dusty stood up and said with tiredness to his voice, "I'm a-gonna get me a little shut-eye. Walker, you're more than welcome ta stay with One-Eye and me. Good night, Miss Aura Lee! See ya in the morn!"

With that said, Dusty turned and headed for the door, but as he opened it and started to step through, he turned around to say one last thing. "Me 'n Miss Aura Lee are a-fixin' ta get hitched." Not another word was spoken. He stepped out the door and gently closed it behind himself.

No one heard him softly humming the song "Aura Lee" or saw the smile of contentment on his face as he looked into the star-filled heavens of an Alaska night.

❧

The Reverend Hill would be making his circuit through Hope the last Sunday of the month, so Dusty and Aura Lee decided to marry on that day, April 30, 1888. It would be the first wedding ever to be held in Hope, and the people were going to do it right.

The church was decorated by the ladies, using lace and brightly colored ribbons in place of flowers. Even though it was the beginning of spring, it was still too early for wild flowers or even fireweed to be blooming.

Everyone in town planned on being at the wedding. Even Johnny Dynamite O'Brien was due up the Cannon Ball with supplies for the town. He, being one of Dusty's friends, would want to attend the wedding. Dusty planned on booking passage for himself and Aura Lee on the *Utopia* to take her to Wrangell and Skagway for their honeymoon. They were picturesque little towns and more settled than other areas they could reach in the allotted time they had. Summers are short and they'd need to return home in time to prepare for the long winter ahead.

This was the last stop for Johnny before his return voyage to Seattle, so there would be plenty of room on board.

*

The days before the wedding went by quickly. When the reverend was spotted on the trail leading to town, it took everyone by surprise. In the past, he usually came by way of boat, with Johnny Dynamite, on the *Utopia*.

Over a cup of coffee at George Roll's general store, the reverend explained why he didn't come by way of boat. He said, "Coming up from Skagway, we had to stop at Homer, on Kachemak Bay. The ice in Cook Inlet prevented us from proceeding up the arm. While waiting there, Captain O'Brien took gravely ill.

"Among the passengers on board was a miner who had once followed a medical practice. He said the captain had acute appendicitis and needed it removed. Then he told us he had not performed an operation in over five years and wasn't sure he could do it. Being the only one around with any doctoring ability, the captain offered him a thousand dollars as a fee, and he agreed to try.

"The only place clean enough to perform the operation was Mrs. Bank's gallery home on the Spit, so without delay, we moved him to it. After liberally applying him with the only anesthetic around, whiskey, the doctor began the operation. The only tools available to perform this were a pair of scissors, a kitchen knife, a forecastle needle and thread, and a bucket of hot water. When the operation was over, the doc didn't give the captain much of a chance. 'I can't do any more for him. Keep him clean, and make him rest. I'm strikin' out for the gold fields,' he said, and then he was gone."

The reverend took a long drink of his coffee and then continued. "One of the other passengers on the *Utopia*, a well-mannered, pleasant, dark-haired man who went by the name of Mr. Smith, said he would watch over him and serve as his nurse until the captain recovered or went under.

"Even though Mr. Smith seemed like a gentle, peace-loving guy," the reverend said, "I sure wouldn't want to upset him. He carries two pearl-handled revolvers under his frock coat, and I got a feeling he knows how to use 'em. To get here in time for your wedding, Dusty, I left on foot the next morning."

Dusty was concerned about Captain O'Brien. His boat, the *Utopia*, was the one he had boarded in Seattle to come north to Alaska. On the voyage, he and the fiery little Irish sea captain had become friends. They had passed long nights at sea, in the wheelhouse, talking of days gone by. As soon as he and Aura Lee were hitched, he decided they would light shuck and head overland to Homer. His friend might need his help, and besides, it was on the trail to Wrangell, Alaska.

CHAPTER 23

If the weather was any indication of how the wedding was going to go, it would be magnificent. The arm was calm and shimmered like a mirror of gold in the early morning sun. It reflected the majestic, snowcapped mountains, and in the azure-blue sky, a great bald eagle drifted on the currents. It was a one-of-a-kind painting by the master that could only be found in Alaska.

The little log church was filled to capacity and overflowing. Reverend Hill was well liked and always gave an uplifting sermon on Sundays. Hope is a God-fearing community, so it wasn't unusual to have the church filled to capacity.

This Sunday, though, was different. The ladies were in their Sunday best, but with a few added touches. Special broaches or other fine jewelry appeared that was brought out for only the most special occasions. Even the little girls had colorful ribbons and lace adorning their hair.

Immediately following the services, the atmosphere changed to one of festivity and anticipation of the wedding to come. No one had seen Dusty or Aura Lee since late Friday, when the reverend had come to town.

Everyone was curious, wondering what they would look like in their wedding garb.

The reverend called the congregation to order, and then the door to the church opened and in walked Dusty and his best man, One-Eyed Reilly. You could have heard a pin drop. The look on everyone's face was worth a thousand words. The two men walking up the aisle looked nothing like the One-Eyed Reilly or Dusty Sourdough they knew. Dusty had traded his familiar buckskins for a gray frock coat and a black tie and, tucked into the top of highly polished cavalry boots, a pair of freshly brushed black trousers. Both the men had neatly trimmed their beards, and it was obvious they had both taken a trip to the creek.

When the two reached the front of the church, the reverend stepped forward, and Mrs. Roll began to play the wedding march on the old church pump organ. Everyone stood and looked to the rear of the church as Aura Lee, on the arm of V.O. Rollie, whom she had asked to give her away because she had no family in Alaska, started up the aisle. The Indian war drums started beating in Dusty's chest the minute his eyes fell on her. Her gown was pure white satin and trimmed with delicate lace. She had an ivory cameo on a red velvet ribbon about her neck, and the bridal bouquet she carried was made of silk red roses.

The ceremony went smoothly until the reverend got to the part, "Dusty Sou—. Dusty," he asked, "what's your real last name? It can't be Sourdough!"

"Well, preacher," Dusty said hesitantly, "I reckon if ya need ta know it ta get us hitched, I'll have ta tell ya. I already told Aura Lee, I ain't in trouble with the law or anything like that. It's just that it's the same name as a famous feller down Texas way, and people kept mistaken me fer him, so I changed it! I'd be right grateful if ya'd keep it ta yourself. Reverend Hill gave his word that he would, so Dusty bent forward and whispered it in his ear.

The preacher took an involuntary step backward when Dusty told him his name. He had a look of surprise on his face, and as he spoke, his voice cracked. After clearing his throat, he finished the ceremony, and it seemed as if everyone had forgotten the incident by the time the reception got underway.

The reception went on all day, and as usual, the food was beyond description. Mrs. Roll baked a beautiful wedding cake, and V.O. prepared an open-pit barbecue of moose and other wild game that had returned since the break-up started. There were fresh-baked cookies and birch candy for the kids along with chocolate-flavored milk to drink. When people weren't eating, they were participating in the competitive games, such as sack races for the energetic and horseshoes for the ones who ate too much.

The whole day was filled with joy. One of the most moving moments was when Aura Lee's entire class presented her with the most precious wedding gift of all.

The children waited 'til last. It took two of the older boys to carry it in. When Aura Lee carefully removed the wrappings from the gift, tears wailed up in her eyes. Dusty put his arms around her, and his eyes too, were puddlen up. There before them was the most beautiful cradle any mother could hope for. The boys, instead of going fishing after school, had taken turns working on the cradle. At the same time, the girls had gotten together and sewed the most precious baby quilt you ever laid your eyes on. One of the girls spoke for the whole class and said they hoped that she and Dusty would have a dozen kids. That made Aura Lee and Dusty blush red with embarrassment.

As the day drew to a close and another page in the life of Dusty Sourdough's trail to destiny was completed, Dusty knew that wherever that trail led next, it would be shared with the love of his life. For better or worse, his destiny would become part of hers. The sun was setting as Dusty carried Aura Lee over the threshold of their new cabin. In the few weeks before their wedding, Dusty had time to finish up the remaining work on it. Thanks to all their friends, it was furnished with all the things they needed to make life comfortable. Someone had slipped away from the festivities early and had a cheerful fire going in the big river rock fireplace, making the cabin warm and inviting to the newlyweds.

Morning comes early for Alaskans, and it found Dusty and his new bride in the kitchen, preparing their first breakfast together. Aura Lee had the bacon sliced and sizzling in a big iron skillet on the cook stove while Dusty was grinding up his special blend of coffee beans.

Aura Lee noticed Shadow Spirit didn't quite know what to make of the new arrangement but she seemed to understand that the two people she loved most in the world were there together, and that suited her just fine. With the smells of breakfast cooking, she had her best lovable puppy look on and Aura Lee's heart melted. She "accidently" dropped a slice of bacon to a very happy puppy.

"Look at that rascal!" Dusty said with a chuckle. "Ya'd think she was spoiled!"

"Dusty, you might fool everybody else, but I've seen you with that wolf-dog, and I know without a doubt that she has you wrapped around her paw. I'm surprised you don't have a place set for her at the table!" Aura Lee tried to keep a straight face when she finished saying this, but when she saw the look of innocence on Dusty's face, she broke into uncontrollable laughter.

During breakfast, Dusty and Aura Lee discussed how they would go overland to Homer. Dusty hoped that Captain O'Brien had survived his operation and was on the mend. The sooner they left, the sooner he could put his mind at ease. Aura Lee could sense the urgency of Dusty's feelings, so she agreed they should leave in the morning, at first light. After all, the trip was her honeymoon too.

The rest of the day was spent making ready for their journey. If everything went well and they traveled at an easy pace, it should take two or three weeks to reach Homer. As Dusty packed grub and other essentials they would need on the trail, he started feeling the weight of responsibility.

"Well, ole girl!" he exclaimed to Shadow Spirit. "We gotta take real special care of our lady on this here adventure we're a fixin' ta leave on." Dusty reached down and gave the great white wolf-dog a loving pat. "Ya help ole Dusty keep her safe, okay."

Shadow Spirit, as if understanding Dusty's words, gave a sharp bark and ran into the bedroom, where Aura Lee was putting a few things in her backpack. By the time they were packed and ready to leave in the morning, the sun was casting the long shadows of evening through the forest and the sky to the west was turning a brilliant red-orange.

Dusty was outside, chopping wood, and Aura Lee was bustling about in her new kitchen. She was preparing a great supper of moose steaks and green beans that she had put up the summer before; boiled potatoes; and for dessert, her specialty, dried apple pie. When Dusty finished splitting and stacking the wood, he rested on the porch, enjoying the panoramic view and the wonderful smells coming from the kitchen.

Whap!

"Dog-gone mosquitoes," Dusty exclaimed. "Those little bloodsuckers are sure enough hungry!"

Whap!

"I reckon we'd better go in before these flyin' critters decide ta pack us off to their lair," he said to Shadow Spirit, who seemed unaffected by the winged pests.

Dusty couldn't remember ever enjoying a better meal, and when he told Aura Lee so, she blushed with embarrassment and changed the subject.

"I sure hope Mrs. Roll don't mind taking over my class while we're gone. Those kids can be a handful at times."

"Ya don't have no need ta fret, darlin'. Mrs. Roll wouldn't have offered if she didn't want to do it, and as far as handlin' them younguns, well, she handles George, doesn't she?"

They both had a good laugh at what Dusty said, and this put Aura Lee's mind to rest. As the flames turned to red, glowing embers in the fireplace, a warm, contented sleep came to Aura Lee and Dusty, cuddled in each other's arms under their warm feather-tick quilt.

Chapter 24

Dusty and Aura Lee woke to a misty, overcast morning. After a hardy breakfast and plenty of hot coffee, the couple hit the trail. Shadow Spirit would run ahead, chasing ground squirrels and frolicking through the forest that existed on both sides of the trail.

The first part of the trail over Resurrection Pass was easy going and pleasant. All the trees and plants that were dormant during the long, cold winter were coming to life with new growth. The abundance of nature was visible everywhere for the eyes to behold. Before noon, the clouds moved out and the sun came shining through in all its glory.

Stopping beside an ice-cold, fast-moving stream for lunch, Dusty automatically looked for any fresh tracks. The usual ones were there—moose, wolf, and Dahl sheep—and then he spotted it. About twenty feet upstream, Dusty found the footprint of a grizzly, imprinted perfectly in the soft mud of the stream bank. This find in itself didn't bother him, but what was bothering him was the freshness of it.

As Dusty stood there, looking at the huge paw print fill with water, he knew it was fresh, very fresh.

Carefully looking about in all directions and at the same time calling Shadow Spirit to his side, he had to make a determination on the bear's intentions.

As Shadow Spirit approached Dusty, her hackles went up and she emitted a low growl from deep within. The scent of the grizzly was strong, and it warned that the bear was close, too close for her liking.

"Easy, girl," Dusty said softly, trying to soothe the big wolf-dog. "Maybe that ole bar' will pay us no never mind and leave us alone. There ain't much we can do except keep a keen eye and hope that grizz don't have a taste for people or wolf-dog. We won't eat lunch here. If that critter gets a snout full of our vittles, we could be in a heap of trouble. Come on. Let's light shuck and get away from here!"

Returning where he had left Aura Lee, he told of his find. She needed to know of the danger and be prepared for what might happen. Dusty could see the fear come into her eyes, yet there was determination too.

"Do you think it will try to follow us?" she asked.

"I reckon not. Anyway, I'm a-hopin' not. That grizz hasn't been out of hibernation too long, and more'n likely, he's a-headin' to lower territories, where spring temperatures are warmer and have made food more plentiful. There are ornery ones though, like that ole rogue that liked the taste of my hide, but I've found if'n ya give 'em plenty o' room, they'll leave ya alone, and that's what we're a fixin' ta do. We'll just have ta be careful."

Before starting up the trail, Dusty listened closely to the sounds of the surrounding forest. He could hear the symphony of spring all about, which was a good sign, for if a grizz was lurking in the dense forest; all the critters and birds would be silent, fearing for their lives.

The sun had made most of its journey across the brilliant blue sky when Dusty found a small spring to set up camp for the night. The site had a tranquil feel to it, and the firewood was plentiful. Not only was there enough to build a cook fire with, there would be enough to keep a cozy warm fire going throughout the night.

How different it was to have Aura Lee along. For a moment, he stood, watching her scurry about, collecting rocks for a fire ring. Then she placed a flat one inside the ring. This was for the coffee pot to sit on and keep warm. Dusty was surprised as well as impressed with Aura Lee's savvy of the wilderness. When Dusty had first laid eyes on her, he thought she was too delicate to know about living in the bush, let alone be willing to do it. Boy was he wrong. She had taken to the trail as a duck takes to water. Aura Lee had a tasty supper ready in no time.

While eating and enjoying each other's company, Dusty kept a watchful eye on their back trail. He was a little worried the smells of Aura Lee's cooking would attract the hungry grizz. When Dusty couldn't eat another bite, Aura Lee started cleaning up and secured the food in a bag so Dusty could cache it high up, in a nearby tree.

Dusty scouted the perimeter of their camp before settling in for the night. He knew that being familiar with the immediate surroundings could mean the difference between life and death. Even though it was spring, temperatures still dropped below freezing at night in the high country. As darkness caught up to the honeymooners, they snuggled close to each other by the cheery fire.

In the far-off distance, a mournful wolf howled and received an immediate answer by a plaintive howl of equal loneliness.

"Gee, Dusty," Aura Lee said sweetly, "that wolf sounds so lonely. Do you think he was calling his mate and she was answering him?"

"Sure, sweetheart. Why, wolves run in packs, like one big family. When ya hear 'em a-howlin', that's just their way of talkin'! Take a look at Shadow Spirit. She knows what they're talking about. I bet she could join right in if she wanted to."

When Dusty mentioned Shadow Spirit's name, she lifted her noble head and looked at him with those knowing eyes. Dusty knew without a doubt, Shadow Spirit did understand everything he said. He also knew that the howling call of the wolves put a longing in the wolf part of her, a longing to return to the wild. Maybe someday she would.

⁓

The night passed without incident, and the morning dawned to a cloudless sky. When Aura Lee opened her eyes, Dusty already had bacon frying on the fire and a cup of coffee in his hand.

"Good mornin', darlin'!" Dusty said. "I figured ya were plumb tuckered out, so I let ya sleep in. Me and Shadow Spirit done took us a look about ta see if'n that grizz might be a nosin' around. We went back down the trail a good five miles and didn't see hide nor hair of that critter. I reckon he decided we weren't worth the trouble."

Dusty and Aura Lee packed their gear after breakfast, returned their campsite to its pristine appearance, and then resumed their trek over Resurrection Pass.

By mid-morning, the couple was above the tree line, and the trail had become narrow and steep. Dusty remembered that the trail led through a high mountain valley, and with a little luck, they could make it by sundown. Dusty again was amazed at Aura Lee's grit; she was as rugged as she was pretty. He never had to wait on her, and not a complaint ever crossed her lips.

When Dusty found a small spring trickling between the rocks, he called a halt for lunch. They had a fast meal of jerky, Johnny cakes, and cold spring water. It wasn't too tasty, but it filled the void and it was fast. The trail became even more treacherous as they made their way to the top of the pass. At times, it was nothing more than a ledge on the face of a cliff. It was these times when a misplaced step could mean a five or six-hundred-foot fall to your death.

The going had slowed to a crawl in one of these spots when an ear-splitting scream came from Aura Lee. Dusty reached out for her and missed. In less than a heartbeat, she was gone. He scrambled to the edge and was almost afraid to look over, and then the weak and shaken voice of Aura Lee came floating up to him. His heart leaped with joy. Looking over the edge, he could see his love lying on a ledge about thirty feet below.

Shouting down, he asked her, "Are ya all right? Can ya hear me? Oh, please be all right!"

Aura Lee turned her face upward and giving Dusty a reassuring smile that didn't quite match her voice when she answered, "I…I think so, but I'm…I'm scared to move. Can you…I mean, how are you going to get me off this ledge?"

As Dusty listened, he could hear the fear in her voice. He too felt the same fear, but to dwell on it now could mean disaster. He swallowed hard, and, with a voice of confidence, he answered, "I'll get ya up here. Don't ya trouble your pretty little head about that. Ya just stay put and ole Dusty will have ya out of this here fix in a shake of a hound dog's tail."

With that, Dusty stood and carefully dropped his pack and began a quick search. Looking about, he spotted what he needed. Just above the trail and to the left was an outcrop of rocks. Taking his faithful lazo off his pack, he looped it around what he hoped was the most secure rock of the bunch. Then he tugged on it with all his weight, and thankfully, it held…so far.

After telling Aura Lee to protect her face, he dropped the lazo over the side. He told her to tie it around her waist and he would pull her up. The next thing that happened changed his plans completely. With a shaky voice, she told Dusty that she didn't know how to tie a knot that would hold and when he started to explain how to do it he realized she could still make a mistake in tying it and it could come undone half way up. The only thing left was for Dusty to go down and get her, but just how he could do that, he wasn't sure. All he knew was that he had no choice. He had to do it. Taking the rope in hand, he eased himself over the edge and slowly worked his way down. As he reached the precarious perch Aura Lee was clinging to, the solution to his problem came to him.

Holding the rope with one hand and reaching for Aura Lee with the other, he told her to get on his back and hang on tight. He wasn't sure he had the strength it would take to climb the rope with her on his back, but he could think of no other way.

By the time he was halfway up, his arms and shoulders were burning from the strain. Looking up to see how much farther he had to go, dirt and rocks came raining down in his face.

"Hey," Dusty shouted, "Shadow Spirit, settle down up there! You're kickin' rocks down on us!"

All of a sudden, they were violently jerked about, and it took all of Dusty's willpower to hang on. Next came a blood-curdling roar. In that instant, Dusty knew they were trapped. He couldn't hang there indefinitely, and he didn't have the strength to go back down with Aura Lee on his back.

The giant grizz roared again and took another swipe at the rope. If he caught it clean with one of his claws, they were goners.

❧

Shadow Spirit had gone a short distance ahead when she'd heard the faint sound of Dusty's voice and then the grizzly's first roar. She sprang into action, sprinting full tilt back down the trail. Without slowing a step, she charged the grizzly and caught it completely by surprise, and the tenacity she attacked with threw him off balance. The grizzly had no equal in the forest, and to have this wolf-dog attacking instead of running in fear was confusing to him. Again and again, Shadow Spirit lunged at the bear, and he backed up. The fur was flying, claws flashing in the sunlight, the bear's teeth snapping together, but each time, they found nothing but air.

As the intense battle raged on above them, Dusty and Aura Lee clung to life just a few feet below, unable to see the fierce battle taking place or do anything about it.

The bear caught Shadow Spirit a glancing blow that knocked the wind out of her. Not knowing that he had only knocked the wind out of her, he moved in for the kill. Reaching down for her neck with gaping jaws, he couldn't pull back fast enough to avoid the lightning speed of Shadow Spirit's razor sharp fangs, which embedded themselves around the bear's nose.

The startled grizzly roared in pain and bolted backward, tossing his head, trying to dislodge the pain that had attached itself to the end of his nose. Disorientated with pain and not being able to shake Shadow Spirit's grip, the bear continued to try to back away from the excruciating pain, tossing his head back and forth and side to side. The final attempt came with one last violent shake of his massive head. He felt the hold loosen and took another step backward, not knowing it would be his last.

Dusty took a chance and looked up. What he saw caused an involuntary gasp to come out of him. Right above them, on the edge, was the bear's back paw, and then, in the same moment of realization, he saw the entire grizzly coming toward them. Dusty's reflexes took over at that point. With everything he had left, just as the plummeting bear went roaring by, he pushed sideways with his legs, and the bear bounced off the ledge that had saved Aura Lee's life. The mighty thud and his enormous weight demolished the small outcropping as he continued his headlong fall to death.

Dusty's adrenaline was going wild, and it gave him the added strength he needed to pull himself and Aura Lee up and over the edge. Laying there on the narrow trail, completely played out, they didn't move. Dusty looked at Aura Lee's dirty, tear-streaked face and thanked the Lord once again for his divine protection. After a few more moments, he rose to his knees and looked around. Blood was everywhere, along with big hunks of bear fur. When he spotted Shadow Spirit's still, blood-splattered body, his heart skipped a beat and a lump came in his throat. Lurching to his feet, he cried out, "Oh no!"

Reaching her side, he dropped to his knees and gently lifted her big head into his lap. "Shadow... Shadow Spirit," he said with an emotion-filled voice. "Ya gotta be all right. There are a lot more trails we haven't traveled or sunsets we ain't seen yet." Closing his eyes, trying to hold back the tears, Dusty didn't see the great wolf-dog's eyes flutter open.

"Dusty," Aura Lee cried out with joy, "she's alive! Look! Look! Her eyes are open!"

Through tear-blurred eyes, Dusty looked down at his brave-hearted companion. She looked a mess. Her beautiful, white coat was covered with blood, but as Dusty checked her over, he found only a few wounds. Most of the blood had come from the grizzly.

"Well, girl, ya ready ta hit the trail?" he asked Shadow Spirit, and then, turning to Aura Lee, he asked, "How 'bout you? Are ya up ta coverin' more ground?"

"We can't get to Wrangell sitting here," she answered, adding, "Let's light shuck!" and they both burst out laughing at her attempt to sound like Dusty.

Chapter 25

Even with Aura Lee's fall and the close call with the grizz, Dusty and Aura Lee managed to make it to the high mountain valley, which had been their goal for the day. The ice on the small lake had already given way to the warmer spring days. The snow that made this route impassable in the sub-zero winter was almost nonexistent with the only exception being the deep, shaded areas where the direct sun couldn't reach.

Dusty picked a campsite that over looked the picturesque lake and valley. He dug out some fish hooks and line and told Aura Lee where to find some bait and then sent her down to the lake to catch dinner. That way, he knew she would take it easy and yet feel useful. By the time Dusty had the camp set up and a cook fire going, Aura Lee had caught four beautiful rainbow trout, not one weighing less than two pounds.

Dusty cut four willow limbs about a half inch in diameter and three feet long to cook the catch on. After cleaning and seasoning the fish, he secured each one on a willow and propped them over the fire to broil. Dusty hoped Aura Lee was impressed by his cooking skills and the tenderness he showed her. He wouldn't let her lift a finger to help with the supper preparation or the cleanup afterward.

The next day, they decided to spend another day resting in the majestic splendor and solitude of the magnificent valley. As the day slipped by, they roamed the different game trails around the lake. Dusty showed Aura Lee some of the plants and roots that were edible and grew in abundance in the wilderness. The day ended all too soon for their liking, and after dinner, as they snuggled under their blankets, Mother Nature gave them one last display of her awesome beauty: the Aurora Borealis. They drifted off to sleep while the lights danced in the velvet blackness.

The next four days went by uneventfully, and on the fifth day, they reached Skilak Lake and camped where a sparkling creek emptied into it.

Dusty decided to build a raft and travel the length of the lake and then raft down the Kenai River, where it exits the lake. It took Dusty almost a week to gather the materials and build the raft.

On the day Dusty finished building it, an old prospector/explorer named Dickey came paddling up the lake in a canoe. Upon seeing smoke from their fire, he came ashore and enjoyed Dusty and Aura Lee's hospitality. While on the trail, contact with other humans was rare, and the opportunity to share news from the outside with one another was an occasion to savor. Over steaming cups of hot coffee, they listened to the news he had picked up at the Trading Post in Kenai.

He told them of the parts of the river that could be dangerous on their way down and to watch out for some bushwhackers that were robbing people. They spent most of the day in conversation, and after supper, Dusty invited Dickey to spend the night in their camp. He accepted, but at first light, when Dusty rolled out of his blankets, he found that Dickey was long gone. Maybe he didn't like good-byes.

After breakfast, it didn't take long to pack up and load their belongings on the raft. When Dusty called Shadow Spirit and tried to get her on the raft, she would have nothing to do with it. Finally giving up, Dusty told her to follow by land as best she could.

Dusty, with forethought, had rigged a makeshift sail out of a blanket. With a good breeze pushing them along, it was no time before the mouth of the river came into view. As they approached the outlet, he dropped the sail, and as Aura Lee folded it up, he unlashed the mast, and casting it adrift, he picked up the pole he had made for navigating the river.

Around mid-afternoon, they came upon the first serious set of rapids. However, long before these treacherous rapids came into view, the low, heavy rolling sound of their danger was audible. Both Dusty and Aura Lee were apprehensive about entering them, and when Dusty guided the raft toward shore, he could see the relief fill Aura Lee's face.

He decided to have a look before starting down this first set. Securing the raft in some quiet water, Dusty and Aura Lee followed the river downstream. The sounds of rapids were worse than the reality of them, and the channel looked wide and deep enough to allow the raft through without much danger.

Returning to the raft, the couple ate a late lunch and then pushed off into the fast-moving current and headed for their first experience through white water. As the raft picked up speed, Dusty shouted, "Hang on! This is gonna be one rip-roarin' ride!"

Aura Lee saw his lips moving, but his voice got lost in the sound of the churning, crashing water that swirled about them. Dusty didn't need to worry about Aura Lee hanging on. The minute she saw the rapids close up and personal, she grabbed a piece of rope and tied herself to the raft. The rapids were much worse than they had looked from the shore. As the raft careened down river, being tossed about like a cork, Dusty gave up trying to steer it. Instead, he used his pole to push away from rocks. A direct hit on one of these could easily shatter their raft.

With a sudden lurch, the raft breached the river, and before Dusty could do anything about it, the downstream side of the raft got caught under the churning water and became violently tipped on its side. Dusty felt himself flying through the air and, in the next moment, with a splash, found himself being pulled under by the raging river. With his lungs about to burst, he fought for the surface. Which way that was, Dusty wasn't sure.

The current had a hold of him and tossed him about like a twig. When his head broke the surface, he gasped for air and immediately slammed his head against a huge rock. Dazed, the river pulled him under again.

At that point, the river widened out and became very docile. Aura Lee had to stop the raft, and this was as good a spot as any to try. With rope in hand, feet first she jumped off the raft and found the water barely knee deep. Wading ashore with the raft in tow, she quickly secured it to a nearby tree and headed upriver.

She hadn't gone two hundred yards when a noise caused her to freeze in her tracks. She hadn't thought about the dangers that might be lurking in the woods when she left Dusty's Hawkens on the raft. Now, as the thought occurred to her, it was too late. Swallowing hard, she held her ground as the sound came closer.

"Well, whatever or whoever you are, come on out and show yourself!" she yelled at the approaching noise. On that command, to her relief, out bound Shadow Spirit, with her tail wagging. "Oh, Shadow Spirit," she cried, sobbing and holding the great wolf-dog close.

"You were wise to follow us on land instead of going on that raft. Dusty's gone! Come on, girl. Find Dusty. Find him, Shadow Spirit. I know you can."

As she pleaded, the great animal could sense Aura Lee's urgency. Without waiting for a further command, she turned and bound up the river with Aura Lee close behind. They hadn't gone far when, up ahead, Shadow Spirit came to a sliding halt on the riverbank and danced around, excitedly barking. When Aura Lee caught up, her fears became reality. There, lying half in the water on the muddy river bank, was Dusty.

His face had a terrible bruise down the side, and from where she stood, it didn't look as if he was breathing. Rushing to him, she calmly called his name, "Dusty?" "Dusty, please answer me!" she cried.

Reaching down, she took his arms and tried to pull him farther up the bank. On the first tug, water came gushing from Dusty's mouth, then a choking cough, accompanied by a groan. With much effort, Aura Lee rolled him on his side, and the rest of the water came pouring out, followed by more coughing.

"Wha-what happened?" Dusty asked feebly. "I feel like a herd of caribou ran through the middle o' me! There ain't a part a me that didn't get stepped on." Reaching up, he touched his face and wrenched with pain. I shor' nuff went fer a swim. I shoulda fallered your lead and tied myself on. I'll know better next time!"

"Next time?" Aura Lee asked with disbelief in her voice. "You're not getting back on that…that raft!" she said more as a statement than a question.

"Why, shor I am! It's like gettin' throwed from a hoss. If'n ya don't get back on, ya'll be a feared of it the rest of your life." Dusty didn't wait for any more questions. He got wobbly to his feet and headed down river.

The rest of the day they spent drying out their gear and making repairs on the raft. Dusty was in obvious pain but never once said a thing about it. It was a foregone conclusion in the wilderness. Unless you were completely incapacitated, you kept moving.

Shadow Spirit stayed by Dusty's side until he and Aura Lee boarded the raft the next morning. Again, she refused to ride the river.

With the new pole Dusty had to cut, he pushed off and headed into the main current. The river, at this point, widened out and meandered lazily through awesome canyons and dense evergreen forests. From time to time, an eagle would swoop down on the river with his razor-sharp talons and, with perfect timing, pluck an unsuspecting fish from its depths.

A variety of wildlife was also in abundance, from the smallest creature to a ferocious grizzly.

When a big bruin lumbered out of the woods, it took Dusty and Aura Lee by surprise, and for a moment, they thought it might come after them. Much to their relief, the bear only gave them a casual glance, and then he went about the business of getting himself a drink.

The slow-moving current and warm sun made for a comfortable day as they floated down the river. By nightfall, the couple was close to the confluence of the Russian and Kenai River. It was then that Dusty smelled wood smoke, and as they rounded a bend, a small Indian village came into view.

Dusty was apprehensive as the current pulled them toward the village and the excited, waiting Indians.

As the raft bumped the bank, the Indians swarmed around them, terrifying the wits out of Aura Lee. Dusty took hold of her hand and gave it a reassuring squeeze. The Indians began closing around them even tighter, with menacing looks on their weathered faces. Dusty didn't blink or back up, and when they became completely silent, he knew that whatever was going to happen, it was about to take place and how he handled it could mean the difference between life and death.

Dusty knew not to show fear as a tall, resplendent Indian stepped forward. His commanding presence left no doubt in Dusty's mind this was the man in charge. Dusty also knew that a man's eyes say a lot about him, that they truly are the windows to your soul. When his and this powerful-looking Indian's eyes met, he could see strong determination as well as kindness in them. They were the color of cold, gray steel, but the smile lines around them softened and gave the impression that he was inwardly smiling at Dusty.

Ever so slowly, Dusty let a smile come to his lips, and in return, the Indian started smiling too. In that instant, the tension disappeared and everyone started talking at once.

To Dusty and Aura Lee's surprise, several of the natives could speak English, and in no time, they were sitting around their campfire, sharing information about the river. The chief told them that less than one sleep away, the river became very treacherous and it would be impossible for the raft to pass over it. He offered the use of one of their skin-covered river boats and said that when they reached Kenai, they could leave it at the trading post and one of his men would pick it up later.

☙

The next morning, Shadow Spirit gave the Indians quite a start as she came charging into camp. If it wouldn't have been for Dusty's quick reflexes, one of the natives would have taken a shot at her, but Dusty saw what was happening and, in an instant, put himself between the wolf-dog and the surprised native. After Dusty explained about Shadow Spirit, the morning returned to normal and the couple prepared to leave.

The skin-covered boat was a definite change for the better. It maneuvered surprisingly easily and it was quite sturdy. When they approached the rapids that the Indians had told them about, Dusty's stomach started to knot up. With his near-drowning still fresh on his mind, he wasn't sure he wanted to deal with the white water. He thought that maybe it would be easier to portage around it, but down deep inside, he knew that he was deceiving himself. For the first time in his life, he felt real fear, and if he didn't face it head on, it would be with him the rest of his life. After coming to grip with this, he swallowed hard and pointed the boat into the main channel, and with a shout, they shot down the river.

At the trading post in Kenai, Dusty and Aura Lee met Captain Swanson. He was the owner of the trading post. After explaining about the boat the Indians had loaned them, Dusty asked about a ship sailing south. To their disappointment, they had just missed the *L.J. Perry*, under the command of Captain Lathrop. She had sailed on the morning tide and was the last ship expected until the end of the month.

With this news, the only other choices they had were by foot or horseback, so they headed for the stable at the end of town. There, with any luck, they would find horses they could buy and they could continue their journey to Homer on the trail to Wrangell.

Chapter 26

After securing two saddle horses and one pack animal, Dusty and Aura Lee found a two-story building made of rough-cut lumber and logs that passed for the town's only hotel. The rooms were small and sparsely furnished. They had a bed, a dresser, and a washstand with a basin and a pitcher of water sitting on it.

Dusty surprised Aura Lee by having a large copper bathtub brought to their room, and after the desk clerk made several trips to the kitchen, it was filled with hot water and lots of soapy bubbles. This was a luxury not often afforded a lady on the Alaska frontier, so she took full advantage of it while she could and soaked in it for an hour.

After a long bath and a restful nap, supper was in order, so Dusty and Aura Lee went looking for a place to eat. Not far from the hotel, they spotted a sign on the front of a grub tent that read: "Beef Steak Dinner with Fried Taters & Hot Apple Pie, 4 bits (Coffee Extre)." The words *beef steak* were all Dusty needed to read.

"Shucks!" Dusty exclaimed. "I ain't had me a beef steak since a-leavin' Seattle. Come on, darlin'. Let's go wrap ourselves around a couple of them there steaks afore headin' south." It was hard for Dusty to believe they had real beef in Alaska, but when they got inside, sure enough, it was real beef.

The grub tent owner, a jovial, rotund gent, said, "Some of the original Russians that settled the area had brought cattle with them from Russia. When Russia sold the territory and pulled out, some of them decided to stay on and raise cattle. The only thing is, because of all the interbreeding, the cattle are getting smaller. That's why I have ta charge so much for a steak."

Whatever the reason for the price of the steak, it didn't matter to Dusty. As soon as he took the first bite, he forgot all about the cost.

Dusty and Aura Lee woke to a drizzly, gray morning and found that the temperatures had dropped dramatically. After a hardy breakfast of fried ham, eggs and potatoes, and scalding-hot coffee to wash it all down with, he and Aura Lee headed for the livery stable.

As the two walked down the boardwalk, Shadow Spirit appeared from nowhere, barking and wagging her tail in an excited greeting.

"Where ya been hidin'?" Dusty asked as he reached to stroke the wolf-dog's head.

He knew that Shadow Spirit probably slept in the woods outside town. She didn't like town or strangers, so when they got close to a town, she always slipped away. But how she knew when they were headed down the trail was still a mystery to Dusty, but then again, she was always doing unexplainable things.

Even though the day was gloomy and gray, the couple had a grand time. The well-marked trail made travel easy, and the miles went by quickly. The horses were trail wise and had an easy gait. To Dusty's surprise and pleasure, Aura Lee was a fine horsewoman. By suppertime, they had covered half the distance to Kachemak Bay. Without a doubt, they would reach their destination sometime tomorrow in the late afternoon.

The next morning, Shadow Spirit, with an impatient bark, let Dusty and Aura Lee know that she was ready to hit the trail. The sky, an azure blue, promised to bring a picture-perfect day for travel. In no time, they were overlooking Kachemak Bay and the small settlement of Homer.

It wasn't hard to find Mrs. Banks's gallery on the Spit, and when they arrived, she had good news for them. She said that just yesterday, with the help of Mr. Smith, Captain O'Brien was moved back to his boat. That meant that the captain was on the mend and the life-threatening danger was past. After thanking Mrs. Banks, the couple, with Shadow Spirit by their side, headed down the Spit to find the *Utopia*.

The boat, tied up at the dock, looked all but abandoned, and as they approached, Dusty, in an attempt to attract someone's attention, yelled out; "Yo, on board the *Utopia*!"

After a moment, a tall, thin, dark-haired man wearing a black frock coat stepped from the captain's cabin and introduced himself as Mr. Smith. He said he had been attending Captain O'Brien through his recovery and then invited Dusty and Aura Lee on board.

The captain greeted them with a big smile and congratulations on their marriage. Dusty could see the pain in his eyes, and his pale skin color gave away his charade of well-being. When he said he was ordering the *Utopia* to get underway tomorrow on the morning tide for Seattle, his voice was weak and didn't have the normal crispness.

"Are ya sure yur ready ta make the voyage?" Dusty asked with concern in his voice.

"Of course I am!" answered the captain with some of the old fire in his voice, and to emphasize that the subject was closed, he asked Mr. Smith to have the crew assemble on main deck at noon.

The captain said that he needed to rest, so Mr. Smith showed Dusty and Aura Lee to their quarters below deck.

At noon, with the help of Mr. Smith, the captain, with much pain, made his way to the main deck to address his crew. He told them to make ready to get under way on the morning tide. The crew showed their malcontent with this order by mumbling amongst themselves. If the captain could have seen the devious looks they gave each other, he would not have returned to his bunk, trusting that his orders would be carried out.

The next morning, Dusty and Aura Lee slept in, and when they awoke, they were surprised to find the boat still tied to the dock. Sensing that something was wrong, Dusty quickly dressed and told Aura Lee to lock the door behind him and stay in the cabin. Grabbing his Hawkens and checking the load, he headed for the captain's cabin. On deck, he ran into Mr. Smith, who was also heading for the captain's cabin with a great deal of concern on his face.

After knocking several times and receiving no answer, they opened the door and walked in. Upon hearing the door open, Captain O'Brien woke with a start. "What's goin' on? Why ain't we movin?" He yelled, "This is mutiny! Mr. Smith," then he said in a calm voice, "may I borrow those pearl-handled Colts you keep under your coat?"

"Of course, but what will I use?" Mr. Smith asked. "Dusty and I intend to back you, but not empty handed."

"Over there in the cabinet, next to my desk, you'll find a twelve-gauge shotgun. The shape I'm in, I couldn't handle it. But I'm sure you can." Lurching to his feet, the captain headed to the main deck with Dusty and Mr. Smith close behind.

As the trio approached the ladder leading to the main deck, a form appeared at the end of the passageway.

In the blink of an eye, the captain had one of the pearl-handled Colts out and leveled at the man he recognized as the first mate. "Hey," he shouted at the man, "turn around real slow, you son of a sea urchin, or by thunder, I'll blow ya into the next life!"

The man turned slowly, and the fear on his face was unmistakable. He started to speak, but the captain interrupted with a harsh, "Shut up! I'll do the talkin'. If you don't get this boat underway immediately, I'll hang you or anyone else from the yardarm. Is that clear?"

"Ye-Yes, sir!" he stuttered.

"Now get!" the captain ordered in a commanding voice.

The first mate turned and ran up the ladder in relief and fear for his life.

It was slack tide when the *Utopia* slipped away from her berth in Kachemak Bay. The tension on board was so thick that you could cut it with a knife, and the first mate could look no one in the eye.

Aura Lee stood at the rail, drinking in the surrounding beauty of the picturesque bay as the *Utopia* glided over the calm, azure-blue waters. The great white wolf-dog sat at her feet, and when she jumped and began to bark and wag her tail excitedly, Aura Lee turned and looked in the direction that had Shadow Spirit's attention. She broke out in joyous laughter and patted the wolf-dog on the head, saying, "Oh, Shadow Spirit, you can't go play with that cute little sea otter. If you jumped in the water, you'd scare the poor little thing to death. And besides, he can swim better than you!" Aura Lee laughed again and reached down and playfully ruffled Shadow Spirit's soft, white coat.

The days on board the *Utopia* were blissful and serene, and the weather couldn't have been more perfect. The evenings could find Aura Lee and Dusty strolling the deck hand in hand or just sitting by the rail, with Shadow Spirit by their side, watching the night sky that was aglow with the light of a billion stars.

Even Captain O'Brien seemed better. Being at sea was like medicine to him, and every day, his strength grew. On the final day of the voyage, he appeared to be his old, commanding self, right down to his freshly brushed uniform and the jaunty tilt to his sea captain's cap. He announced that we would be making port in two hours and to prepare to disembark immediately upon arrival. He pointed to some ominous clouds building over the snow-covered mountains to the east. He said a storm was blowing in. He could feel it on the freshening wind.

Wrangell seemed peaceful enough. The dock area was buzzing with men loading another steamboat called *The City of Seattle* with bales of furs that would eventually be made into fashionable coats for wealthy Easterners and Europeans.

As Aura Lee stepped down the gangplank, the men on the dock stopped their work. A few made remarks that were off color, and Dusty fixed them with a mean look that made them turn away. Dusty had a bad feeling about the place and wished they hadn't decided to stay over a day or two before going on to Skagway. Even Shadow Spirit walked with her hackles up and her senses on full alert.

If Dusty would have known what Wrangell, the town some said was worse than any lawless town in the Old West, was like, they would have never stepped foot off the *Utopia*.

CHAPTER 27

It had been sometime since Dusty had been in a town that had all the earmarks of trouble, but that one had them all and more. Between the dock and the hotel, Dusty and Aura Lee saw four fights and thought they were going to be in the middle of a gunfight when two hard cases came flying out of one of the many saloons along the main street.

The only thing that stopped the two from grabbin' iron was a tall, thin man with a sweeping, bushy mustache. He was wearing a flat-crowned, black hat and frock coat. In an instant, he stepped up to one of them and busted the unsuspecting man over the head with his six-gun, which seemed to just appear in his hand.

The man was unmistakably the law. He had a marshal's badge on his vest, and it was obvious that he knew what he was about. But there was something else, something that was familiar to Dusty.

The hotel was a typical frontier hotel, adequate at best. The only redeeming thing about it was the small but clean restaurant located in the lobby.

As the couple entered, the aroma of the food increased Dusty's appetite twofold. "I'm as hungry as bear," he said. "I sure do hope they have plenty of grub back there in that kitchen."

"I'm sure they do, darling," Aura Lee said sweetly with a smile on her lips.

Dusty loved her smile, and it always made his heart skip a beat, just as it did the first time he saw it on her beautiful face. He put his buckskin-clad arm around her shoulders and guided her to a table on the far side of the room. After sitting her so she could look out the window, Dusty put himself with his back against the wall so he was facing the door. He slowly slipped his Colt from the holster so no one would notice and laid it carefully beside him on the bench. He didn't much like the feel of the town, and he wasn't going to take any chances.

The waitress confirmed Aura Lee's beautiful but sensitive nose when she said the supper special was beef stew and freshly baked bread. It sounded good to both of them, so Dusty ordered three portions, two for himself and one for Aura Lee.

As the waitress left to place their order, the marshal who stopped the gunfight earlier stepped through the door. He stood there a moment and surveyed the room. His eyes missed nothing, and when they met Dusty's, a flicker of familiarity came to them. It was at that instant that Dusty remembered who he was and where he had known the marshal from. A smile of recognition came over the marshal's face, and he quickly crossed the dining room and was standing in front of their table, reaching to shake Dusty's hand and saying, "Why, Dusty…Dusty T—"

Dusty sprang to his feet, interrupting the marshal. "Sourdough!" he said a little too loud, "Dusty Sourdough. Shaking the marshal's hand, he noticed that everyone in the restaurant was watching them, so he quietly asked the marshal to join them. "Marshal, I'd like ya ta meet my wife, Aura Lee."

"It's a pleasure to meet you, Marshal," she said.

"The pleasures all mine, ma'am, but my friends call me Wyatt."

"This is the famous Wyatt Earp," Dusty said to Aura Lee. "We did some marshalin' together back in Dodge City a long time ago." For a brief moment, Dusty's mind drifted back to those ruff-and-tumbling days of yesteryear when a young man knew no fear.

"Well," said Wyatt, "ya finally settled down and found you a wife, and a right pretty one too. I never thought you'd find a woman that would put up with your cantankerous ways."

The trio had a good laugh at Wyatt's comment. Then Dusty invited the marshal to dine with them, and he graciously accepted.

The conversation over supper was congenial and filled with old times. Over hot apple pie, the talk turned to the present, and as Dusty and Aura Lee said their good-byes, Wyatt turned to Dusty and said with a serious tone to his voice, "Why don't you come by the office in the morning? Seein' how you're here in Wrangall, maybe I could get you to help me out."

The next morning, before sunup, Dusty slid out of bed and lightly kissed Aura Lee on the cheek, trying not to wake her. He loved to watch her sleep, and that morning was no different, but that morning, he had something else to do. Strapping on his Colt, he silently slipped out the door and down to the hotel lobby. The restaurant was open, so he walked in, sat down, and ordered a light breakfast consisting of toast and a mug of steaming black coffee. Dusty noticed a couple of hard cases sitting a few tables away. There was something familiar about them, but Dusty couldn't figure out just what.

When he got up to leave, the one who was facing him let his hand slip down to the butt of his tied-down Colt. Dusty didn't let on that he noticed the move. He paid his bill and left the restaurant, never giving a second look to the two gunslingers who were watching him with heightened interest.

"Mornin', Wyatt," Dusty greeted as he stepped into the marshal's office. "What's the something ya wanted ta talk ta me about?"

"A couple hard cases came into town two days ago," Wyatt started. "Maybe you remember them. When we were marshalin' together back in Dodge City, you and I sent a pair of bank robbers to prison for twenty years, Curley West and Lefty Jackson. Remember Lefty had two boys? One was about fourteen and the other around sixteen."

"Yeah. How can I forget? Those boys were trouble even back then, stealin' from the general store and beating up on the smaller boys. They ought ta be full growed by now."

"They are, and they're here in Wrangell!" Wyatt got up and went to a file cabinet sitting next to the one and only cell and pulled out a wanted poster. When he handed it to Dusty, a look of recognition came over his face.

"Why, I seen these two pole cats at breakfast, just afore I came here," Dusty declared. "The Jackson brothers. They turned out just like their pa, no good. This here poster says their wanted fer horse stealin' down Texas way. That's a hangin' offense. Ya reckon they're runnin' from the law or a-huntin' you and me?"

Wyatt thought for a minute and then answered, "They have ta be runnin'. There's no way they could know I was here. You didn't know you'd run into me, and I for sure didn't even know you were in Alaska, let alone Wrangell. No. They're runnin'. We just happen ta be where they're runnin' too."

Dusty and Wyatt discussed what their next move should be, and they both agreed that they should meet the situation head on. Wyatt strapped on his famous Buntline Special, and Dusty checked the loads in his Colt. Both, with a look of determination on their faces, stepped out into the early morning darkness and started up the wagon rutted street to meet their destiny.

Most of the town was still asleep as Dusty and Wyatt made their way toward the cafe. It was hard to believe that Wrangell was such a dangerous place, but Wyatt had said that it was rougher than Tombstone ever thought of being.

Dusty was pondering this and other things Wyatt had told him when a shot rang out from between two buildings to the left of them. It was hard to say who pulled their six-gun faster, Dusty or Wyatt, but when they both fired, it sounded like one thunderous shot.

Then another shot came from the darkness of an alley farther up the street, but before Dusty or Wyatt could return fire, the most horrendous, blood-curdling cry came from the darkness of the alley. They could hear the screams for help from a man that was obviously being attacked by some sort of a wild animal.

Dusty threw a couple of shots in the direction where the first shot had come from and then sprinted toward the alley. By the time Dusty reached the alley, all he could hear was a low, guttural growl and the whimpering, begging voice of a man scared out of his wits. The man had managed to get himself to a temporary place of safety, perched precariously on top of some wooden crates. Standing below him, ears back, growling with teeth bared, was Shadow Spirit.

"Well, well," Dusty said. "Looks like ya treed yourself a real pole cat this time, and by the looks of his arm, he'll 'member you while he grows old in the gray-bar hotel."

Reaching up and jerking the dry gulcher off the crates, Dusty recognized him as one of the hard cases from the cafe. "I guess ya went from horse stealin' ta dry gulchin'. Well, son, you've reached the end of the line. You and your brother are going ta be in the calaboose a good long time."

At that moment, Wyatt came down the alley with the other Jackson brother being pushed along, reluctantly, in front of him. Wyatt's prisoner was holding a bloody arm and protesting every step of the way. The marshal told Dusty that his last volley of shots must have found a target because as Dusty entered the alley after the second shooter, the other pole cat came stumbling out between the two buildings, hollering that he was shot and was giving up.

By the time Aura Lee got up and was downstairs looking for Dusty, he and Wyatt were in the hotel café, talking about old times over a cup of hot steaming coffee.

"Tomorrow," Dusty was saying, "Aura Lee and I will be heading for Skagway for a couple of days and then back ta Hope. We got plenty ta do afore winter sets in. What about you, Wyatt? You fixin' ta keep marshalin' here in Wrangell?"

"No. No, after this morning's ruckus, I realized that this is a young man's game and I'm not young anymore. This little town's as rough as any one I've ever been in, and rougher than most. When I took the job, it was on temporary basis until they could find another marshal. I'll be headed back ta Seattle in the next few days."

When the two old friends said their good-byes on the dock the following morning, there was sadness in both their eyes. They were smiling and joking about seeing each other again, but they both knew that the chances of that were pretty remote.

As the boat slipped away from the dock, the stately figure of a man with the glint of a marshal's badge on his chest could be seen walking away. His head was down, and if someone would have been closely watching, they would have seen him try to blink back a tear that escaped and silently slid down his weathered cheek.

CHAPTER 28

The waters were alive with an abundance of sea creatures, otters, seals, and even an occasional whale or two. The couple stood on deck and talked of the things they would see when they got to Skagway the next morning. When Aura Lee had asked Dusty earlier about the goings-on in Wrangell, he had brushed it aside as if it was nothing. Aura Lee knew better, but she also knew that it wouldn't do any good to go on about it.

The day was wonderful and warm, and Captain Lathrop had invited them to dine at his table for the afternoon meal. While standing at the rail, waiting for lunch to be served, a familiar face approached the couple.

"Why, good afternoon, Mr. Smith. I thought you left on the *Utopia* when she left for Seattle."

"No," answered Mr. Smith. "I decided to stop in Skagway, and the *Utopia* was sailing straight through to Seattle. There was room on board the *L. J. Perry,* so here I am. I heard rumors of a gold find in the Klondike, and everyone headed that way would have to go through Skagway. Maybe I can figure out a way to make a living off them."

"Good luck, Mr. Smith," Dusty said, shaking his friend's hand.

"It won't have anything to do with luck. You can bet on that," Mr. Smith said with strong conviction. "Maybe we'll see each other again. I won't be hard to find. Just ask around for Soapy, Soapy Smith."

Dusty and Aura Lee knew that the time was drawing near when they would need to start for Hope. Already, the sun was setting earlier each day, and soon, the leaves would be changing color and dropping to the ground.

Their honeymoon had been filled with enough adventure to last most people a lifetime, but for Dusty and Aura Lee, it was just beginning. The adventures to come in their lives would be rewarding and never ending. After all, they are on their road to destiny.

Part Three

Chapter 29

After splitting a cord of wood, Dusty decided to head over to the general store and see if his new rifle had come in. It had been four months since ordering it, and he was eager to use the new gun on his next foray into the bush.

The familiar trail heading to Hope was short, and Dusty always enjoyed the walk. The scenery was magnificent, and this was one of Dusty's favorite times of year. Birch and cottonwood trees were changing to their fall colors at a rapid pace, from brilliant yellow-gold and oranges to vivid reds. Small animals of the forest were scurrying about with urgency. They knew that winter was fast approaching. It was just a matter of days before the first freeze. Termination dust had already come to the high mountain passes, marking the end of summer.

Dusty knew Shadow Spirit loved these walks too and was torn between going with him and staying with Aura Lee. After all, Aura Lee was putting up winter stores such as smoked fish and moose meat. With a little coaxing, Shadow Spirit knew Aura Lee would give her a handout. In the end Dusty knew he would win out, the temptation to run and frolic in the woods was more than her desire for a handout.

The trail meandered along a small stream, sparkling like precious jewels. Dusty decided to get a cold drink and was just bending down when the excited bark of Shadow Spirit caught his attention. Turning and sprinting up the trail toward all the commotion, he was stopped dead in his tracks as he rounded a bend in the trail. Not more than ten feet in front of him was a sight that made him double over with laughter. Shadow Spirit had herself a porcupine cornered and wasn't quite sure what to do with it. The bristly little critter didn't have any backup in his nature. Shadow Spirit, to her chagrin, had already found out the hard way. Her nose looked like Aura Lee's pin cushion with several quills sticking out of it.

"Shadow Spirit, I reckon ya better give that critter some room or yer goin' ta have more than just a few of his quills a-stickin' in yer nose. Now get on over here and leave him be!"

Shadow Spirit chose discretion was the best part of valor and gave the porcupine one last halfhearted bark and trotted to Dusty's side.

"Come on," Dusty said. "Let's go back to the stream so we can have some clean water to wash your wounds. I have a feelin' the cold water's gonna feel real good after I pull out those quills your little friend left in your nose."

After doctoring Shadow Spirit's nose with loving care, the pair finally made their way to town without any more mishaps.

Upon entering George Roll's store, Dusty caught the tail end of a conversation between George and a stranger he hadn't seen before. As their conversation was concluded, something caused Dusty to take a second look at the man standing next to the potbelly stove.

He looked like the typical prospector, unshaven, dirty, and carrying a Colt on his right hip slung low and tied down.

A Colt tied down? Wait a minute, Dusty thought to himself. *A prospector doesn't usually have his Colt tied down like a gunslinger.* As Dusty took a closer look, he became more suspicious. Something just didn't ring true about this stranger.

When this suspicious-looking gent turned to leave, he hesitated for just a fleeting moment. His eyes caught Dusty's, and in that brief moment, Dusty thought he recognized the man. And more than that, he thought he saw a glint of recognition come over the stranger as he hurried out of the store.

"Why, howdy Shadow Spirit!" George Roll said, pretending to ignore Dusty completely. "What brings you to my store this fine fall morning?"

With a bark and her tail wagging wildly, she jumped up and put her front paws in the middle of the smiling storekeeper's chest. Shadow liked George, and the feeling was mutual. She knew he always had a pat on the head and a biscuit for her when she came for a visit, and as usual, the storekeeper didn't let her down.

"Did that new rifle I ordered last month come in?" Dusty asked, interrupting the play between Shadow Spirit and George.

"Yep," he answered. "Came in yesterday on the freight wagon from Kenai. She's a beauty too. I reckon it's the latest thing. Who would ever believe there would be a rifle that would fire more than once without reloading?"

"Yes, sir," Dusty said. "This here new lever action Winchester will fire seventeen rounds as fast as ya can work the lever. The army's been using them fer a while, and they think they're the greatest invention since the six-shooter. Who knows? Maybe havin' this new-fangled rifle might save my life someday."

The two friends shared more small talk, and eventually, the conversation came around to the stranger who was in the store when Dusty came in. George said the man went by the name of Jake.

He didn't offer a last name, and keeping with the code of the West, George said he didn't ask him for it. Jake was full of questions about the local miners and who was finding color and who wasn't.

"The strange part of his conversation with Jake," George said, "was he never asked where there might be a good place for him to prospect."

This too struck Dusty funny and added more fuel to his suspicions about the stranger. The Jake character would be worth keeping an eye on.

After getting the few things Aura Lee wanted and a hundred rounds of ammunition for his new rifle, Dusty bid George farewell and stepped into the brisk Alaska fall afternoon.

"Hey, Shadow. Shadow Spirit!" Dusty yelled as he walked up the dirt street, heading for home. "Where has that dern tail-wagger gotten ta now?" he asked to no one in particular. "She can disappear faster than any breathin' thing I ever did see." Dusty knew that it was useless to call her. By now, she could be anywhere, and more than likely, she was already at the cabin, mooching a handout from Aura Lee.

Heading down the trail toward home, Dusty started making plans for his trip into the bush. This would probably be the last one before snow flew. He and Shadow Spirit would leave at first light in the morning and head up Six-Mile Creek. This trip would be different, he thought. This time, not only would he be hunting game for their winter cache; he would be doing it at his leisure. Game had been plentiful all summer, and everyone in Hope had taken enough to insure a comfortable winter. Dusty and Aura Lee were probably the last to be putting up stores for the winter because they had started late, due to their honeymoon.

Dusty's mind drifted back to the trail to Wrangell and the adventure he and Aura Lee had shared. It was in that moment of thought that Dusty was startled back to the present with the snapping of a twig behind him, and he spun around. Dusty couldn't see anything. He knew something was there. He could feel it. He stood stock still for almost five minutes, listening, straining to hear the slightest noise, but none came.

"Well," Dusty spoke softly to himself, "maybe my imagination is playing tricks on me." With that said, Dusty turned and continued his journey home.

☙

As Jake left the store, his thoughts were crowded with faces from his past. He knew he should know the man that walked into the store when he was trying to get any information he could out of the gabby storekeeper. Standing in the wagon-rutted street with the afternoon sun casting long shadows, he watched the wind kick up a dust devil, and in that moment, it came to him. The stranger was a US marshal, or anyway, he used to be. *If the guy…what was his name … Dusty, Dusty what?* The last name just wouldn't come to him, but it would and if this Dusty recognized him, the plans he had would be ended. He had to kill this Dusty, and he had to do it now.

Jake froze in his tracks the moment the twig snapped beneath his moccasin-clad foot. The creek bed paralleling the trail had offered perfect concealment for him to follow Dusty until he could get a clear shot at him. Now he was in danger of being discovered, and he didn't like the idea of facing Dusty head on. Very carefully, he slipped back into the thick forest, thinking to himself, *Another day, Dusty Sourdough. Another day.*

Chapter 30

Shadow Spirit, with her keen ears, heard Dusty long before she could see him. With one bounding leap, she was off the porch and heading across the clearing as Dusty emerged from the woods surrounding their cabin. Dusty dropped to one knee and gave the big, white wolf-dog a hug as she caught him across the face with her big, pink tongue. She danced around him, barking and lunging in mock attack, trying to get Dusty to play with her.

"Come on, girl. Let's go see what Aura Lee has for supper."

Turning and heading for the cabin, Dusty didn't notice Shadow Spirit hesitate and look back down the trail. She had heard something, but her nose could detect nothing out of the ordinary, so she too headed for the cabin.

At supper, Dusty told Aura Lee of his plans to head up Six-Mile in the morning and said that he planned to be gone a couple of days. The winter was fast approaching, and any extra meat he could bring home he said they could use.

After dinner, Dusty and Aura Lee took the big bearskin robe down from the peg by the door and went outside to enjoy the glorious sunset. Dusty had built a swing and hung it on the covered porch for just such occasions. He constructed it out of willows and suspended it from the porch roof beams with rawhide rope so they could gently swing back and forth and watch the millions of stars, one by one, start twinkling in the great north night sky.

The next day started with a good breakfast and plenty of hot coffee. Afterward, Dusty checked his gear and gave Aura Lee a hug and a kiss good-bye and headed toward another adventure on his trail to destiny.

⌒

The climb was long and dangerous, but Dusty knew that the reward at the end was worth it. This was only the third time he had made the journey into this high mountain canyon with towering granite walls and sheer drops of more than six hundred feet. One hasty step in the wrong place could mean a long fall to his death, and chances are no one would ever find him. When Dusty had stumbled onto this canyon, it was pure luck. He had been on a hunting foray into the area above Six-Mile Creek.

The game trails were many, and fresh tracks were everywhere. Shadow Spirit smelled the scent of animals in every direction. For a moment, it confused her and she couldn't decide which trail she wanted to follow. When Dusty saw the fresh tracks of a good-sized moose heading up a trail to the north, he called her to follow. With a tail-wagging bark, she bound up the trail with her nose to the ground. Soon, she was out of sight, running through the deep, lush forest.

The trail at first had sloped gently upward and followed a small stream babbling happily along its way to Six-Mile Creek. The beauty surrounding Dusty never ceased to amaze him; this place called Alaska was magnificent. It made no difference which way he looked; the scene was always awe inspiring.

Dusty walked about for an hour and was enjoying the day when he decided to stop at a stream to get a cool drink of water. Dipping his hand in the crystal-clear water and starting to bring it to his mouth, something caught his attention out of the corner of his eye. It took a moment to spot what it was, but when he saw it, his heart skipped a beat. Reaching down into the icy, cold water, Dusty came up with what appeared to be a gold nugget. He couldn't believe his eyes; at first, he thought it might even be fool's gold. But just feeling the weight of it, he knew better. Without a doubt, it was the genuine item. The nugget was about the size of his thumb. It wasn't the biggest one he had seen since coming to Alaska. It was, however, the biggest one he himself had ever found.

Looking around, Dusty fixed the landmarks in his mind. Later, he could return with his gold-panning gear and spend time working the stream. For now, his priority still had to be game for their winter cache.

With Dusty's mind again fixed on hunting, he wondered what had become of his companion, Shadow Spirit. In late afternoon, when the sun was casting long shadows, the great, white wolf-dog came bounding down the steep and treacherous trail. Dusty didn't know where she'd been, but he was sure happy to see her.

Almost immediately, after leaving the stream where Dusty found the gold, the trail became narrow and rocky. The ascent was treacherously steep at times.

Dusty had to be on all fours as he continued his climb. The tracks he had been following most of the day were now nonexistent and had been for the past two hours. As usual, his curiosity had driven him on, and now, for all his effort, the trail seemed to be coming to a dead end. That was when Shadow Spirit charged back up the trail to where it seemingly dead-ended at the base of a cliff, and right before his eyes, she disappeared. She was gone. Startled by this sight, Dusty struggled to get up to where he had last seen Shadow Spirit.

From below, where he had been standing at the time of her disappearance, the cliff looked unconquerable; it went straight up a good five hundred feet and looked to be as smooth as a sheet of ice. But when he reached the base of it, to his amazement, he found out differently. The trail didn't end after all; instead, it made a sudden dip and then led to a small opening hidden from his view from down below.

He wondered how many men had stopped before they reached the base and found the opening. If his faithful companion hadn't vanished, he, for one, would have never continued the climb.

Very carefully, Dusty slipped into the opening. It was very narrow, but the height seemed unlimited. Looking up, he could see daylight six hundred feet above his head. Dusty had no idea how this phenomenon was formed, but it was an awesome sight. The shaft was overlapped by the outside wall of the cliff, and the entire vertical fissure was concealed from external view.

As he worked his way along, he could hear the wind coming at him from the direction he was moving. It was an eerie, mournful sound giving Dusty the chills, even though the midday temperature was comfortable and warm.

Looking down, he could see Shadow Spirit's tracks in the layers of dust covering the trail. Dusty felt an overwhelming urgency to pass through this spooky place. All he wanted to do was to get to the other side, wherever that was. He noticed, as he moved along, that the trail was not only slanting down but it was getting wider too.

During his headlong rush to reach the other end of the passage, Dusty failed to see the strange formations in the rock walls on either side of him. It wasn't until he stopped to take a short rest and catch his breath that he started looking around at the unusual surroundings.

The eons of time were recorded in the layers of rock Dusty was staring at. As he looked around in wonderment, his eyes spotted something and he gasped. Getting up from his resting place, he stepped toward the towering rock wall to take a closer look at a wide layer of quartz traveling horizontally, waist high, the entire length of the wall.

Dusty knew that gold could sometimes be found in quartz. Stepping back to his worn, old pack, he untied the well-used hand pick he always carried with him on an outing such as this. He would only pick around for a little while, he said to himself. Then he began chipping at the quartz. It was a few minutes later when Shadow Spirit came bounding down the narrow path. She came to Dusty's side for her usual pat on the head and was not disappointed when Dusty stopped his picking and greeted his great white wolf-dog.

"I'll bet you're a-wonderin' what I'm doin' a hammerin' on this rock wall," Dusty said to his faithful companion as if she understood. "Well, girl, I'm lookin' fer gold. I'll only be a few minutes, and then we'll move on. You just rest your paws and take a nap." Chuckling to himself, he turned back to his task.

⌒

Dusty lost track of time and was surprised when Shadow Spirit started barking at him. Turning to ask her what the ruckus was about, he noticed for the first time that the light in the narrow passage was fading, and he had wasted the whole day looking for that elusive dream called gold. "We'd better get ourselves on out of here and find a place to make camp fer the night. Besides, I ain't found one speck of gold. Let's get a-goin'."

As Dusty started down the sloping trail toward the failing light, the sound of Shadow Spirit raising cane back where he had been chipping quartz caused him to turn to see what all the commotion was about.

"Hey! I said we were leavin'," Dusty shouted to the wolf-dog as she danced around some of the quartz he had chipped away that was lying on the ground. Ignoring her excitement, he hollered, "Come on. And where was your support when I was losing interest? Come on. Let's us get out of here."

Reluctantly, Shadow Spirit followed Dusty to the end of the passage that opened into a remarkably green valley. A beautiful but raging river ran through the far end of it, and the spruce trees, abounding everywhere, were surprisingly big. The long winters of subzero temperatures and short summers kept evergreens from growing as big as their cousins to the south, so the size of these trees surprised Dusty.

Making their way along the well-defined trail to the valley floor, it wasn't long before they found a perfect spot to set up camp for the night. After getting a small fire going and their evening meal out of the way, Dusty stretched out by the fire to watch the sunset in all its radiant beauty. Dusty knew Shadow Spirit always loved this part of the day on the trail too, when she could lay next to her master and put her great head on his chest. There, she always received an ample amount of love when he affectionately rubbed her ears until she fell asleep.

Laying there, drinking in the serenity of this hidden valley and listening to the sounds of night critters starting their day, Dusty's thoughts returned to his distracting day of looking for riches when he should have been hunting.

"You know," he said to the dozing wolf-dog, "I've been some kinda fool today, getting caught up in gold fever. I wouldn't mind finding enough to get along with, but, shucks, I have all the riches I'll ever need. I have it all around me every day. I have gold in the morning sun, silver in the millions of stars shining through the darkest night. I have an immeasurable wealth of love from Aura Lee. And you, girl, I can't leave you out. Your loyalty is like a precious jewel that couldn't be bought for any price, ol' girl. How could I ask for more?"

Shadow Spirit lifted her head and licked at the gentle hand that was softly stroking her head.

"I think it's goin' ta be a cold one tonight. Better bank our fire and try to get some shuteye."

After completing this task, Dusty rolled up in his blanket next to the fire, and with Shadow Spirit lying close by, he was soon fast asleep.

CHAPTER 31

Chilled to bone, Dusty woke before sunup. He had underestimated how cold it was already getting in the high country. The light frost on the ground and the crispness in the air told him that winter was fast approaching. He knew that very soon, this valley would be blanketed in the white softness of winter's snow and access to this high mountain sanctuary would be no more until breakup.

Reaching in his pack, Dusty took out the makings for his breakfast and soon had coffee boiling and bacon sizzling on a cheerful burning campfire. By the time he and Shadow Spirit ate, the sky to the east was beginning to show signs of the start of a beautiful day.

As Dusty moved across the picturesque valley with the early morning sunlight casting a golden glow on the changing colors of autumn, he soon found an abundance of tracks. The indication of the variety of wildlife in the valley amazed him. This time of day, along with sunset, were his favorite times of day. The beauty and freshness of a new day always meant that a new adventure awaited him, and all he had to do was embrace it. At day's end, the splendid colors of sunset with the purple glow of twilight were his reward from God for doing the best he could along his trail to destiny.

Squatting down by the stream to examine the assortment of tracks, he found, was almost a fatal mistake. It came without provocation and happened so fast that Dusty scarcely had time to react. The only warning was an almost human, blood-curdling scream, and then the slashing claws and needle-sharp fangs of a forty-pound lynx was on him, trying to rip out his throat. Grabbing the vicious cat by a handful of fur, Dusty tried his best to dislodge the animal from around his neck. The cat screamed and, again, with lighting fast speed, went for his throat. The only thing that saved Dusty's life was the fighting-collar he always wore around his neck. More than once, this Indian device had saved his life by not allowing his assailant easy access to his throat.

The fight raged on, and both man and animal were tiring fast. The cat had gotten some good licks in, but none of the claw marks were serious—yet.

While the two were locked in mortal combat, Shadow Spirit was biding her time to enter the fracas. When the right moment came, she moved with blinding speed. Dusty, knowing that his strength was waning, bunched the muscles in his shoulders and, with everything he had, flung the cat to the ground, but what Shadow didn't know was that this ornery little cat had a little something left for the wolf-dog too.

Going on the attack, Shadow Spirit lunged for this ferocious wild cat and was caught totally off guard by its tenacity. Without any backup in it, the lynx regained her balance and struck out at the charging wolf-dog. Too late, Shadow saw the paw, with claws flashing in the sunlight, come slashing toward her. The wolf-dog's forward momentum wouldn't allow her to stop in time to avoid the sharp pain the cat administered to the end of her nose as she slammed into the fierce little cat. Shadow's weight and speed knocked both of them off balance and the two rolled head over paws in a cloud of dust. The scrappy lynx gained her feet first. She ignored the growling wolf-dog and casually sat down on her haunches and started cleaning her beautiful fur coat. This move perplexed the noble wolf-dog and caused her to look curiously at this little bundle of dynamite. She barked and growled and even faked a charge at the cat, but the lynx acted as if the wolf-dog and the man didn't exist.

After Dusty was on his feet, he regained his rifle, took careful aim, and started to squeeze the trigger. At that instant, Shadow let out a howl, causing him to look away. This proved to be a mistake. Whether or not the lynx knew she was in mortal danger remains a mystery, but at the precise moment Dusty looked away, she casually got to her feet, turned, and walked off into the brush without a backward glance. Surprisingly, Shadow Spirit didn't charge after her. Instead, she looked at Dusty as if to say, "Well, why didn't you stop her?"

"If that ain't the dog-gondest cat I ever seen," Dusty exclaimed. "She acted like it was just a game she was a-playin' and tired of it. If that don't beat all. Doggone cat!"

After attending to their minor wounds and
gathering up all the gear strewn in every direction
during the fracas, Dusty and Shadow Spirit continued
along a game trail leading down the valley.

In the afternoon, Dusty stopped for lunch and was unpacking his coffee pot when Shadow's low growl got his attention. Looking in the same direction as the wolf-dog, Dusty couldn't believe his eyes. Not more than twenty feet away, that "doggone" cat had crept up on them and was just sitting there watching and waiting, but waiting for what? The lynx, showing no fear, leisurely stretched out on her front paws and was content to watch from afar.

Now, seeing a lynx in the broad daylight is a rarity in itself because by nature, they are a shy critter. To have one intentionally come this close to man was unheard of. Dusty was perplexed, to say the least, with the strange actions of this cat. Shadow Spirit had stopped growling and was having a staring contest with the feisty little feline. Then Dusty, for no reason other than curiosity, dug out a piece of jerky from his pack and started to approach the little predator. As Dusty got closer to the lynx, she rose to her feet and emitted a low, hissing growl.

"Easy, little one," Dusty said with a soft, gentle voice. "I ain't gonna hurt ya. I only want ta give ya a little somethin' ta eat."

Continuing to talk softly, Dusty moved closer. The cat stopped her low growl and hissing when the human got within arm's reach. As the man reached out with something in his hand, the aggressive little cat's curiosity got the best of her. As she stretched as far as her body would allow, without moving her feet, the scent of jerky overpowered her fear of man. Reaching out, she took the morsel of dried meat and immediately backed away from the human.

"Well, what do ya think?" Dusty asked the fierce little cat. "It's pretty tasty, eh? And it's a lot less painful for the both of us if ya take a likin' to it instead of my hide!" Chuckling to himself, he turned, gathered up his gear, and started up the trail with Shadow Spirit by his side.

By late afternoon, the valley trail had led Dusty to the northernmost reaches of the valley. Twice, he had had a clear shot at game and decided not to take it. The silence in the valley was so peaceful that he didn't want to break the serenity of the day by the booming roar of his Winchester. Stopping by a pool formed by a splendid waterfall, which originated above a tall, rugged cliff, presented a formidable barrier, and Dusty knew that if he wanted to go any further, he would have to find another way.

The churning, swirling water had a hypnotizing effect on Dusty as he sat on a large rock and looked down into the rushing river. It was Shadow Spirit's playful barking that brought him back to the problem at hand. Turning to see what her excitement was all about, he almost fell into the pool with uncontrollable laughter. That doggone lynx was back and giving Shadow Spirit fits. She was sitting on a limb just out of reach of the wolf-dog's futile leaps. The antics Shadow was going through were hilarious, and Dusty couldn't help noticing that the cat was only playing. When she would take a swipe at the wolf-dog's nose, her claws were retracted, so no pain was administered when, on occasion, she would connect with the bouncing black nose.

"Well now," Dusty said, "if that don't beat all. I do believe those two have made friends. Shadow Spirit,"

Dusty called, "is that your new friend? Don't ya know you two are supposed ta be deadly enemies?"

With her tail wagging, Shadow bound to Dusty's side, and he could see the excitement, not anger, in her eyes. Glancing up at the lynx, he saw that she showed no fear or anger either.

As Dusty was observing all this, he could tell by the curious look the cat had when he pat Shadow Spirit on the head, he was having a hard time understanding all that was happening. Dusty offered him a bite of jerky that was probably strange tasting to her, but she cautiously took it anyway. Even when Shadow Spirit was playful and friendly toward him, he was leery but didn't back away from the cavorting this *should be* enemy was displaying. For some unknown reason the cat showed no real fear and even seemed almost comfortable around him and Shadow Spirit.

Ignoring the pesky, strange acting cat, Dusty decided to stop for the night and started to make camp.

CHAPTER 32

Stopping early for the day gave Dusty a chance to relax after pitching camp, so he decided to try his luck fishing for his dinner in the swirling pool beneath the waterfall. The lynx and Shadow Spirit were still playing and taking turns chasing each other around the camp.

Finding just the right willow for his pole and getting his line and hooks out of his possible bag, Dusty quickly put together his fishing tackle. The last thing he needed before sitting down to some serious fishing was bait, and this was simple to find. That is, if you knew where to search. As Dusty looked about for the right spot, he spied an old, rotten log jutting out of the bank just a short distance from the falls. The bank at this spot had several rocks and boulders strewn about, and the water splashing from the falls kept them constantly wet and slippery.

Who's to say what Dusty was thinking about, but whatever it was, his mind had to be on something else other than the task at hand. Otherwise, he would have seen the tree root sticking out of the bank just far enough to catch his foot. One always needs to be aware of everything around. The slightest let up of this number one rule of the wilderness could and undoubtedly would result in irreversible tragedy. At that moment in time, Dusty was about to find out just what price he was going to pay for breaking that most important rule.

Dusty's foot caught the root just as he was reaching out to the old log. He was right when he guessed that it was rotten, for when he grabbed at it to stop his fall, it gave way and he and the old rotten log went headlong into the churning, rushing water beneath the falls.

The water was so unbelievably cold that it took Dusty's breath away. It took a moment for him to realize that the undercurrent was pulling him deeper and deeper into the depths of this swirling pool. With all his strength, Dusty pulled for the surface. With lungs about to burst and heart pounding in his ears, his efforts finally paid off and his head broke the surface. Sucking in the deep breath of air his lungs were screaming for, Dusty realized he was in trouble, serious trouble. He could hear Shadow Spirit's frantic bark and hoped she wouldn't jump in, in a valiant effort to save him. But if she jumped in to save him, she too would surely drown.

The current was pulling at Dusty's legs. It was a sucking feeling, and he knew that it was about to pull him under and there wasn't a thing he could do to stop it. The cold was numbing, and his arms felt like lead. He struggled for one last deep breath as the surging water pulled him down, down into what he thought would be his watery grave. He was vaguely surprised the water was pulling him almost straight down. In his mind, he thought and hoped that as it pulled him down, it would push him away from the falls, but it wasn't. Instead, it was pulling him straight down in a vortex that didn't seem to have any bottom. He felt something hit his shoulder and then his head, his leg, and his head again. His lungs were screaming for air, and in the instant before slipping into the blissful cocoon of unconsciousness, he had the strange sensation that he was falling through air, not water.

A roaring sound came to Dusty's ears as he opened his eyes. But wait! He opened his eyes, and it was as if they were still closed, or blind, or dead. Reaching up to his face, he could feel that his eyes were open. Dropping his hands, he could feel the rocky ground beneath his outstretched body. *What's going on? Where am I?* He didn't feel dead. He felt wet. The last thing he could remember was his lungs screaming for air and then the soft, enveloping blackness taking over, and the blackness was still with him accompanied by bone-chilling cold. Groping for his possible bag, he was surprised to find it still strapped over his shoulder and across his chest.

Searching through the bag, he found what he was looking for. In the soggy mess that used to be his possibles for the trail, he took out an oilskin that had been carefully rolled up and tied with sinew so no water could saturate it. Dusty fumbled with the knot that was holding it together. Loosening it, he unrolled the small bundle and was immediately rewarded with what he was looking for: dry matches and a nest. Feeling around, he found a rock and struck the Lucifer on it.

In total darkness, the small flame from the match seemed like a bonfire. Looking about, he saw he was in a vast cavern and had been washed upon the bank of a fast-moving underground river.

"Ouch!" Dusty exclaimed, blowing out the match, plunging the cavern back into total darkness. Striking another one, Dusty quickly looked about for any driftwood he could find. Reaching for nearby pieces, he got them into a small pile before the second match went out. This time, when he struck the third match, he hastily held it under the wood where he had placed the small nest. Almost immediately, to Dusty's relief, the small twigs burst into flames. As the little fire grew, Dusty found more driftwood to add to it until the fire was blazing brightly and it illuminated the cavern with its warm, glowing light.

Looking about, Dusty concluded that somehow, he was miraculously spared from death. The roar he had heard when he regained consciousness was coming from the upper extremes of the cavern. In the outermost edge of the firelight, he could see where the roar was coming from and, in all probability, he surmised was his method of entry to this underground river. A column of water not much wider than his body was cascading from the cavern ceiling with tremendous force. The tower of water had a blue-green glow to it, probably caused by the light from above. As best Dusty could figure, the waterfall he was camped next to, over eons of time, wore through the bottom of the pool, and a portion of the water coming over the falls started draining into this underground river. In time, the creek Dusty had followed up the valley would get smaller and smaller as the hole in its bed enlarged until it would eventually disappear completely.

Dusty's concern at that moment, however, wasn't the course of the creek but how to get out of this trap he found himself in. Obviously, he couldn't go back the way he had come, so he had to find another way, and those alternatives were limited, very limited. As far as he could see, there was only one choice, and that was down river. How far he could get depended on a lot of unknowns. For one, the amount of ceiling clearance there was above the river. If the clearance closed down and he had no room to keep his head above the water, he would have to hold his breath until it opened up again or he would drown. Of course, the other big question

Dusty didn't even want to think about was whether or not the river even had an exit to the surface. With the thought of drowning and escape in mind, Dusty devised a plan that he hoped would help him stay afloat on his journey down this dark, foreboding river.

Finding a small log that had washed ashore, he cut several strips of fringe from his buckskin shirt and tied them together. After making two long lengths, he wrapped them around the log, making handles to hang on to in the swift current that would try to separate him from his makeshift float once he entered the water.

Digging around in his possible bag, Dusty came up with a soggy hunk of moose jerky to eat and sat down to ponder his attempted escape from the cavern. He knew he could be free in a matter of minutes, or it could go the other way. He could be plunged deeper into the bowels of the earth with no hope of seeing the light of day again. In short, Dusty knew there wasn't a guarantee that the river would surface soon or if it would even surface at all.

Waiting or thinking about it wasn't going to get him out of the fix he was in. When he had finished his meager meal of jerky, Dusty stood; took hold of his log; and eased himself into the cold, swirling water.

The swiftness of the river surprised Dusty. Glancing back at the fire he had left burning for its light, he was amazed to see it was already just a little pinpoint flickering in the far distance. The river, after taking a sharp turn, was again plunged into total darkness.

At times, his legs dragged the bottom, and in narrow spots, he would brush the rocky sides of the subterranean passage. The darkness in itself was unnerving, but when the sound of rapids reached Dusty's ears, his blood turned as cold as the river. Either the river was going deeper into the earth or hopefully it was just the natural drop of the land causing the sound of rapids.

Rounding another sharp turn, Dusty was suddenly dropped about six feet and, for an instant, was pulled under the surging water. He was thankful he had tied the buckskin strips around the log. Holding tightly to them, the log dragged him to the surface and allowed him to get a gasping breath of air before he was shot through a series of brutal, rock-strewn rapids. The beating Dusty was taking was beyond words.

He could sense the walls and ceiling of his rocky prison closing in on him. Letting go with one hand and reaching scarcely above his head for a fleeting second brought a startling discovery. The top of the cavern was just inches above his head, and at any moment, that could disappear. By now, Dusty had swallowed more than his share of water, and the coldness of this subterranean river was starting to take its toll.

Dusty could feel a pronounced change in the current. He wished he could get a Lucifer out of his possible bag so he could have enough light to get a quick look around. This, he knew, was wishful thinking because any minute, the calmer waters could change and the fight for survival would be on again. Dusty was sucked into the next peril. There wasn't any warning, not the roar of rushing water or anything to indicate the hazard ahead. As deceiving as the calm water had appeared, and barely having time to catch his breath, he was pulled under and into a vortex of rushing water. The small log he had been using as a float was ripped from his hands as he plummeted along at an alarming rate.

Dusty didn't have time to do anything except try to protect his head from the pounding the rest of his body was taking. The lack of air was making him feel lightheaded. Even when he saw a faint light, his dulled mind didn't immediately register it. He was on the verge of passing out and knew that he was facing death when an incredibly sharp pain wrenched his entire body. A crushing blow to his back and an intense bright light hit Dusty. At the same instant, he was spewed from his underground trap. At first, looking around, Dusty couldn't comprehend where he was. The lack of air and the bone-chilling cold had dulled his mind. But there was something familiar about this place where the underground river had ejected him.

Treading water in a small pool, not unlike the one where his incredible journey had started, Dusty shook his head and tried to clear it. He tried to figure out where he was and how long he had been trapped in the underground cavern. The position of the sun told him it was midday. But was it the same day? Or had more than a few hours passed? How long had he been lying unconscious in the cavern earlier before coming to and building a fire? How many miles had he traveled down the surging underground river?

Putting these thoughts aside, he struggled to the bank and pulled himself out of the bone-chilling water. With his teeth chattering uncontrollably, he immediately started gathering makings for a fire. Again, he was thankful he had been able to hang onto his possible bag. Reaching in it, he pulled out the oilskin that kept his Lucifers dry. Again, the oilskin had done its job. The stick matches, thankfully, were dry. Striking one on a nearby rock, it flared to life in a cloud of sulfur smoke. As the fire blazed, the warmth gave Dusty new life. After taking off his buckskins, he hung them on branches near the fire to dry. Standing in his long johns as near the warm fire as possible, steam commenced to rise from them almost immediately, and in no time, Dusty was starting to feel dry.

The day was passing quickly, and his stomach told him he needed nourishment. This being the driving force, Dusty started looking about the surrounding forest for anything he could eat. He knew it would have to be wild berries because all he had for a weapon was his knife, so any kind of game was out.

Starting up a faint trail leading away from the river, Dusty was quickly rewarded with several bushes of wild blueberries. Ravenously, he stripped the fruit, and as the first handful hit his mouth, he barely tasted the sweetness of the succulent morsels as they headed for his growling stomach. Dusty was so busy taking care of his insatiable hunger that he failed to hear a strange noise coming from farther up the trail until it was too late for him to have a chance to get away.

Turning with his knife in hand to face this horrendous sound, Dusty stood with feet wide apart and awaited his fate.

CHAPTER 33

Dusty couldn't believe his eyes. That terrible sound was coming from a human. That's right, a human, and a pretty humorous-looking one at that.

He looked like an old prospector and had short, bowed legs; an almost-snow-white beard; and his twinkling blue eyes were looking over a pair of round spectacles sitting on the end of his nose. He looked to have a gentle nature, and when he spotted Dusty standing there in his long johns, his rotund belly shook with laughter, and he asked, "Hey, pilgrim. Did ya ferget somethin' when ya left home this mornin?" Then he thought his question was so funny he almost fell over laughing at his own joke.

"What's so funny?" Dusty shouted so he could be heard over the laughter. "My breeches and shirt are over yonder, dryin' by my fire!" Dusty said, trying to sound dignified, but the laughter coming from this jovial little man was infectious, and Dusty couldn't contain himself any longer.

Both men were laughing so hard they didn't see the great white wolf-dog come lunging at Dusty until she had knocked him down.

The stranger, not knowing this was a greeting of great joy, mistook it for an attack. He pulled the rifle he was carrying up to his shoulder and shouted, "I'll get the critter. Push it off ya so's I can get a shot!"

"No, no!" Dusty shouted. "She's friendly. She's mine. Don't shoot!"

Dusty kept hollering, "Enough! Enough!"

But he was laughing so hard that Shadow Spirit could barely understand him. When she did, she broke away, running in circles, yapping and barking with an unmistakable joy that at last, she had found her master.

In all the excitement and joy of his reunion with Shadow Spirit, Dusty had completely forgotten the stranger until he heard him saying, "The name's Kuskokwim, Kuskokwim Jim! I have a summer place through the pass over yonder," he said in a friendly voice as he pointed back at the pass that Shadow Spirit had just come across.

"Howdy! I'm Dusty Sourdough, and that crazy-actin' wolf-dog is Shadow Spirit. I'd offer ya a cup, but I'm afraid the best I can do is offer a warm place next to my fire to sit a spell."

As Dusty and his new friend walked the short distance to his fire, Dusty tried to explain what had happened to him, and as he did, Kuskokwim listened with a strange look on his face. When Dusty had finished telling his story, the prospector stood up and, not saying a word, went to his pack and took out the makings for a pot of coffee.

This puzzled Dusty, and when the friendly little miner ambled down to the stream for water, he still hadn't said a word. Dusty was beginning to wonder if his new friend had heard a thing he had said. Kuskokwim sat the coffee pot on the fire and slowly turned so he was looking Dusty square in the eyes. His gaze felt to Dusty as if it bored into his innermost being. It made Dusty mighty uncomfortable, and when the old-timer started to speak, the sound of his voice startled him.

"I heared tell in an Indian village north of here 'bout a feller who kilt a grizz with his bare hands. I figgered it was just one of them tales that growed bigger and bigger each time it was told and didn't put much store in it. Why, shucks, that there feller has the same name as yours."

He waited, with a questioning look on his face, waiting for Dusty to deny that he was one in the same that the hard-to-believe tales were told about.

When Dusty started to speak, nothing could have prepared him for what he was about to say. "Well, seein' you are supplyin' the coffee, I guess I'm obliged ta tell ya the facts of those yarns a-goin' around."

The stranger sat there with gaping jaws as Dusty unfolded his whole story. When he had finished, there was a new look on Kuskokwim's face. At first, Dusty thought it was the look of disbelief, but then, when the little prospector spoke, it was as if he were speaking to royalty.

"I do apologize for funin' ya the way ya looked when I come up on ya. If I'd of known who you were, it sure would have been different, I mean you're a legend, sir.

This embarrassed Dusty something fierce, and all he could say was, "Shucks. It weren't nothin'. You would've done the same thing if'n you were in the same fix and there's no apology necessary. I put my pants on the same way you do."

By now, Dusty's buckskins were close to dry, and to change the subject, he stood up and started dressing, saying, "I reckon I better start a-lookin' fer my gear so's I can try and finish my hunt and get on back to the cabin."

"I can take ya right to that place you spoke 'bout. If'n we light a shuck, we can get there by this time tamarree. That is, if'n ya don't mind me a-comin' along."

By mid-afternoon of the next day, the two men and Shadow Spirit approached the giant waterfall where Dusty's latest adventure had started. All seemed peaceful until Shadow Spirit's warning growl. Both men froze in their tracks. Dusty looked in the direction the wolf-dog's nose was pointing and, at first, didn't see what she was growling at. Kuskokwim jerked his rifle to his shoulder, and at that same moment, Dusty saw what he was aiming at. The miner's rifle went off with a roar just as Dusty sprang forward, knocking Kuskokwim to the ground.

"Hey! What in tarnation did ya go 'n do that fer? I had that cat dead, and ya went and made me miss!"

"I know, and I'm right sorry too," Dusty said apologetically as he offered his hand to help the furious miner to his feet. "Ya see," Dusty said hesitantly, "I know this is gonna sound silly, but that there lynx is a friend of mine and Shadow Spirit's."

The anger slipped from Kuskokwim's face, and in its place, a slow grin started to appear. "Do ya mean ta tell me that varmint snarling and a spittin' over there is a pet?"

"Well, not exactly a pet. We got acquainted along the trail a few days back. His name's Dog, short for Doggone Cat!"

That was all Kuskokwim could stand. He started roaring with uncontrollable laughter and rolling around the ground, grabbing at his sides with delight. When he regained control of himself, he sat up, scratched his beard, and looked seriously at Dusty, saying, "I reckon ya are the feller them stories are about. They say ya can make friends with most of the wild critters in the woods. I wouldn't have believed it, that is, 'til now."

Dusty and Kuskokwim watched Shadow Spirit and Dog wrestle around and growl at each other in mock combat for a few minutes, and then Dusty dug around in his pack and pulled out fishing gear.

"I reckon there should be some fish in that devil river over there," Dusty said, pointing down the river from where he almost lost his life.

"There shor-a-nuff is!" exclaimed Kuskokwim. "I've caught more than my share of some mighty tasty rainbows right over there where you're a-pointin'."

❧

Kuskokwim was right. Dusty pulled out four beauties while the little prospector got the fire going and the coffee to boiling. After an enjoyable supper of broiled trout, beans, and coffee, the two frontiersmen talked awhile and spoke of their wives waiting at home for them. In the morning, they would head for Kuskokwim's cabin and hope, with a little luck, that they would come across the game Dusty needed for his and Aura Lee's winter cache.

As the two new friends talked awhile after eating their evening meal, Dusty knew that the seeds of a new friendship had been planted.

"Well, tamarree comes early, so I reckon I'll be a-gettin' me some shut-eye." With that, Kuskokwim got up from the fire, rolled out his bedroll, pulled the tattered old wool blankets over his head, and was fast asleep.

Dusty laid in his bedroll for a long time as the fire turned to amber coals. Shadow Spirit came and lay down beside him, and Dusty reached out and stroked her soft, white coat. The great wolf-dog let out a sigh of contentment and closed her eyes.

"Old girl," Dusty said softly to the dozing animal, "I guess we both made new friends on this little adventure. Who'd ever believe a wolf and a lynx could become friends? I just hope you won't be too disappointed if Dog decides to stay here rather than follow us back home. Besides, Aura Lee might get a mite bit upset with us fer a-bringin' home a wild ornery cat like Dog."

Dusty glanced over at his companion and saw that she hadn't heard a word he had spoken. She was fast asleep, and sometime during Dusty's one-sided conversation, Dog had silently slipped up next to Shadow Spirit, and he too was fast asleep.

Dusty reached over and poked at the dying embers of the campfire and watched the thousands of tiny sparks race toward the heavens. The billions of stars that blanketed the velvet black sky of the Alaska night made Dusty feel small, like one of the many sparks that had disappeared almost as fast as it had been born. If he hadn't seen them with his own eyes, they might very well have never existed at all.

How insignificant we are, Dusty thought to himself. *We're kinda like them sparks. Few people, if any, ever see them, and then they disappear into the heavens before anyone knows they were around. I guess if a feller really wants ta make a difference, he has ta make enough noise ta be noticed. Otherwise, he'll just get lost among all the other sparks and vanish with time.*

Dusty lay there, pondering this revelation, and watched a shooting star blaze across the northern sky. It made him think of his precious Aura Lee and how she always made a wish when she saw a falling star. He wondered what she had been up to this day, and a strange feeling came over him, an uneasy feeling of foreboding.

Chapter 34

Several times, as she busied herself about the cabin, for no apparent reason, she caught herself looking out the windows and checking the tree line around the cabin. She had never been uneasy before when Dusty was gone, so this was a new feeling to her. She caught herself wishing Shadow Spirit had stayed behind. If something or someone was lurking in the woods, Shadow Spirit would have been able to warn her. With that thought in mind, it dawned on her what she was feeling. Was it a pair of unseen eyes watching her? If so, who could it be? What did they want?

"Oh dear!" she cried aloud, wringing her hands. "This is foolish of me."

Aura Lee tried to take her mind off this scary feeling she had. She sat down at the desk Dusty had built for her and struggled with some of the preparations needed for the new school year that was about to begin. This ploy worked for a short time, but when she got up to put the tea kettle on the fire, she glanced out the window and, for a startling moment, thought she saw a fleeting shadow duck behind a tree just beyond the clearing.

Surprisingly, she felt very calm. Now she knew her imagination wasn't running away with her. She had seen something. Calmly, she walked over to the Colt hanging on the peg by the door and checked its load and action, just as Dusty had taught her. Reaching for her shawl, she threw it about her shoulders and headed into the kitchen. She got her shopping basket down from the shelf next to the bread box and tucked the six-shooter inside, hidden from sight but still easily reachable. She would look like she was going shopping, she thought to herself. When she reached town, she would get help and come back. Then, whoever was lurking out there, scaring the wits out of her, would be on the short end of the stick.

Starting down the trail, Aura Lee tried to look normal and it took all her willpower not to bolt into a full run. Whenever the trail made a sharp turn she'd glance back, trying to see any movement that would indicate someone following her. Once she was sure she saw a man duck behind some alder brush just as she was glancing back.

By the time Aura Lee reached town, she was out of breath and visibly shaken. Almost in tears, she burst into George Roll's store and blurted out, "Someone is sneaking around our cabin, and Dusty is hunting up Six-Mile Creek!"

"Calm down, calm down," George said in a gentle voice. "Tell me, what's this all about? Who's sneaking around your place?"

"I don't know." She sobbed.

George walked to the front window and looked down the street toward the church but saw nothing.

"Well, there's no one there now," he said. "But some mighty peculiar things have been happin' around here lately. Just yesterday, that card dealer over at Scotty Watson's place in Sunrise, turned up missin'.

"Clancy, the saloon keep, said it was the strangest thing. Johnny, Johnny Champbell, the gambler, went up to his room for a nap, 'cause there was supposed ta be a big game that night. He said he wanted ta rest some before it got started. Later that night, Clancy went up to wake him fer the game, and he was gone. All his belongin's were still there, even his six-gun. No one saw him leave, and his horse is still in the stable. The cook said he thought he heard two men arguin' around four o'clock, but he couldn't be sure who it was or what they were arguin' about. The day before that, Curley, up on Bear Creek was jumped while he slept, and all his gold was taken."

"Dusty has been gone awhile, and I have this terrible feeling something awful has happened to him. He's in trouble!"

George could see that Aura Lee was near hysterics, so he gently put his arm around her shoulder and guided her to the bench by the old pot belly stove. He sat her down and then called to the back of the store for his wife.

When Mrs. Roll stepped from the back room and saw Aura Lee and how distraught she was, she immediately took charge of the situation. George, like all men, was thankful and relieved when his wife took over the easing of Aura Lee's mind. He knew she was in good hands, and if anyone could calm Aura Lee down, his wife could. He glanced out the window as he turned to go back to what he was doing, and it was at that moment that something or somebody moved in the woods behind the church.

He quickly reached behind the counter and grabbed the pair of binoculars he kept back there for watching eagles. He focused them on the woods where he thought he had seen movement. He looked carefully but saw nothing move. At first, he was going to chalk it up to his active imagination, but something nagged at him. He took another look. Everything he saw seemed normal. The day was bright, the sky was blue, and there wasn't even as much as a whisper of a breeze.

"Wait! Wait a minute!" he said excitedly as he ran out the door.

He covered the short distance to the end of town quickly, and it only took him a moment to find what he was looking for. There in the soft dirt next to a big spruce tree was a footprint, or rather, a boot print! He squatted down and examined it closely and realized that not many men around Hope, or even all of Alaska, wore boots like what had left that print.

When George returned to the store, Aura Lee was standing by the window and his wife was helping a customer.

"What did you find?" Aura Lee asked calmly. "Was someone following me? Was I right?"

"Slow down. Take it easy. You weren't imagining anything. I found tracks right where you said you had heard something. Now I have to fess up," George said reluctantly. "At first, I didn't think your story held water, but when I saw a cloud of dust with my binoculars and then realized it was a perfectly calm day, I had to go have a look."

George explained that he followed them for a short distance to the creek and then lost the trail because he couldn't find where they came out on the other side. What he didn't tell her was that they looked similar to the tracks left behind up on Curley's claim by whoever the low-down thief was that had robbed the old-timer of his gold. Something told him to keep that piece of information to himself until Dusty got back.

"Aura Lee, I think you should stay here in town with us 'til Dusty returns!" Mrs. Roll said firmly, leaving no room for argument.

"That's very kind of you, but I…I wouldn't want to impose," Aura Lee said politely.

"Nonsense!" George said. "Now you go along with the missus. She'll get ya all fixed up. I'll be along for supper after I close the store."

The room looked neat and orderly, and this surprised Aura Lee. The Rolls weren't known for their neatness. The store was always cluttered with stacks of merchandise everywhere in no apparent order. When George was asked for a particular item, it invariably astounded the customer when the unorganized storekeeper could go directly to the right pile and come up with the item asked for. With these thoughts going through her mind, it made her think of Dusty and how opposite he and George were. Dusty always wanted things neat and orderly.

She smiled to herself, and then, without a warning, a cold chill went through her. A sensation of despair came over her, one that made her feel or sense in her heart that Dusty, at that very moment, was in a life-and-death situation.

CHAPTER 35

Dusty awakened before daylight with Aura Lee on his mind. He had a bad feeling concerning her before he fell into a fitful sleep, and now that he was fully awake, it was still with him. He pulled his blanket up tight around his ears against the frosty cold of the early morning and felt Shadow Spirit stir at his feet. Without a doubt, winter was almost here.

Kuskokwim came out of his blankets as cranky as an old Grizzly that had been woken up early from his winter hibernation. "Can't a man get a full night's sleep around here?" The old prospector growled. "It ain't even daylight yet. How's a body supposing ta get his beauty sleep?"

"I'm sorry," Dusty said apologetically. "I can't stop worrying about my wife. I fear something is going on and she needs me ta be there!"

"I reckon ya need ta head on back and come a-callin' when you've put your mind at ease."

After a quick breakfast and gathering up his gear, Dusty shook hands with his new friend and headed down the trail with Shadow Spirit leading the way. Traveling downhill, they made good time. By lunch, they had covered better than half the distance back to Hope. Dusty wasn't hungry, so the rest stop lasted only a few minutes, and then he and Shadow Spirit were on their way again.

It was early nightfall when Dusty and Shadow Spirit made it to town. The evening cook fires were lit, and the smells of home cooking made Dusty's mouth water and his stomach growl. Dusty decided to stop by George's store and pick up a little something for Aura Lee before heading out to the cabin.

"Howdy!" Dusty said over the ringing of the cowbell attached to the door. "What's new around—"

But before he could finish his question, Aura Lee came bursting into the room and threw her arms around his neck and started sobbing big, deep sobs. Dusty held her tight and gently stroked her hair until she calmed down and then he looked down into her tear-stained eyes and asked, "what's the matter, darlin'? Did someone hurt ya? If...if," he stammered, and then, before he could finish what he was about to say, George interrupted him and explained what had been happening since he had left for his hunting trip.

When the storekeeper had finished filling Dusty in on all the happenings around Hope and Sunrise, he decided to leave Aura Lee at the store another night. He and Shadow Spirit would return to the cabin alone.

It was totally dark as Dusty approached the clearing where the cabin sat. The night was nippy, and he looked forward to getting a warm fire going. As he stepped into the clearing, he froze at the sound of a low, warning growl coming from Shadow Spirit. He stood there at the edge of the clearing, listening to the night sounds and straining his eyes to see whatever had caused Shadow Spirit to growl.

"What is it, girl?" Dusty asked his faithful companion in a low whisper. "Go check it out, girl."

Shadow Spirit slipped off into the darkness without a sound. Dusty decided to wait a few moments, and then he would circle the clearing and approach the cabin from the back. As he started out, a crashing sound came from the west side of the cabin. Throwing caution to the wind, Dusty jacked a round into the chamber of his Winchester and charged across the clearing. As he got close, he could hear a tremendous scuffle going on. The sound of snapping teeth and humanlike cries made him think Shadow Spirit was in a fight for life. When he rounded the corner of the cabin and got close enough to join in the fracas, he stopped short and broke out in uncontrollable laughter.

"Hey, you two!" he shouted. "Break it up! You guys scared the tar out of me, carrying on like that." Upon hearing Dusty's command, Shadow Spirit stopped her rough-housing, and her new friend Dog backed away, not knowing what to expect. Shadow Spirit gave one last bark as the little lynx slipped off into the darkness.

"I guess your friend follered us back," Dusty said with a chuckle. "Now it's gonna take a heap of talkin' ta convince Aura Lee that that cat decided ta adopt us."

After the fire started blazing, Dusty stepped into the kitchen and opened up a jar of canned salmon. Then he cut off a slice of bread and made himself a quick sandwich. The remainder of the fish he dumped into a bowl and set it out on the porch and said to Shadow

Spirit, "I hope the right critter comes fer that. I'd hate ta attract a bear or some other ornery animal."

Dusty sat in his chair next to the fire and ate his sandwich while pondering all that George had told him. He thought of the stranger who was in the store the day he had picked up his new rifle. Something was mighty familiar about him.

Dusty sat by the warm fire, dozing, and finally blew out the lamp and headed up the stairs to bed. He was missing his Aura Lee, and even though he was exhausted, he had a hard time falling asleep. When sleep eventually overtook him, he had fitful dreams of the days of yesteryear in the Old West. Several times, he would wake up with a start and listen with strained ears, trying to hear whatever had awakened him. When dawn started to break, Dusty got out of bed, as tired as he was when he had crawled into it the night before.

After a hot cup of coffee and a quick bite to eat, Dusty decided that he would travel lightly and only carry his possible bag and rifle. Retrieving his possible bag from the peg by the door, he went into the kitchen to replenish it. Reaching inside, his fingers brushed across the gold nugget he had found.

"Shucks! I fergot all about this," he said as he took out the thumb-sized nugget. "It sure enough is a beauty. I wish I could have found a few of its cousins. This bag's a mess, full of sand, and everything in it is water logged. I might just as well dump 'er out and start all over." With that, he turned it upside down on the plank table in the kitchen.

"Wow!" He could hardly believe his eyes. What he thought to be sand in his possible bag wasn't sand at all. It was gold!

Through cold, beady eyes, the man calling himself Jake watched from his place of concealment, and when Dusty headed for the trail leading out of town, he decided not to follow him. He knew where he was headed anyway, and besides, he didn't want to take any chances on that fool wolf-dog spotting him. He knew that before he could make his move, he'd have to get rid of that pesky wolf, and tomorrow morning wouldn't be too soon.

CHAPTER 36

Dusty wanted to tell Aura Lee of their good fortune, but he decided that he would first search the surrounding woods for any signs of an intruder. He had a bad feeling about all that was happening, and the sooner he got to the bottom of it, the better he and everyone else would feel.

Dusty and Shadow Spirit moved slowly through the dense forest. The great wolf-dog sensed that they were searching for something, so she was on full alert, constantly testing the air for any scent that didn't belong there. As they approached a ravine running along the south side of their clearing, Shadow Spirit's hackles went up and her ears went back as a deep-throated growl came from her. Dusty tensed and looked toward the brushy ravine in the direction Shadow Spirit was pointing.

The only other warning was a puff of smoke and the sound of a shot shattering the early morning stillness. Dusty dived for cover just as several more shots came from the same direction. Bullets were buzzing by mighty close, and Dusty knew that he was in a bad place. He had to find better cover or whoever was shooting might get lucky and hit him. He rose slightly to have a quick look around and was surprised when no shots were fired. Carefully, he showed more of himself until he was standing at his full height. Still, no bullets came buzzing at him. The woods all around were deadly silent. It looked like whoever opened up on them had cleared out. Cautiously, Dusty moved in the direction where he had seen the puff of smoke when all the shooting started.

"Come on, girl. Let's us have a look-see and try to figure out who was a-usin' us fer target practice." Slowly, with his rifle ready, he approached the alder brush where he had seen the puff of smoke. Turning to speak to Shadow Spirit, Dusty was taken by surprise not to find her at his heels.

"Shadow Spirit…Shadow Spirit…" It wasn't like Shadow Spirit to run from danger. Knowing this, Dusty carefully retraced his steps. Approaching the spot where he had been when the shooting started, he heard a weak whimper from the brush to his right. Listening for a moment, he called out Shadow Spirit's name again. This time, he pinpointed the exact location and charged into the brush.

What he found nothing in the world could have prepared him for. There, lying in a small clearing, was Shadow Spirit. She had been shot.

Dusty dropped to his knees and gently lifted her great head. Her eyes fluttered open, and she tried to rise.

"No, girl," Dusty softly spoke, barely able to hold back his tears. He frantically looked for the wound and was horrified when he saw the gaping hole in her hip. Getting both arms under her, he carefully picked her up. Looking down at his beloved wolf-dog, he now was unable to control the tears running down his leathery cheeks.

Dusty headed down the trail toward town, moving as fast as he dared. Shadow Spirit lay limp in his arms until he mounted the steps of the general store. She tried to lift her head but was too weak from the loss of blood.

When Dusty burst through the door, George was busy filling an order at the counter, but seeing the limp body of Shadow Spirit, he cleared the cluttered counter with one fell swoop of his big arm. "Put her here," he said with concern. "What happened? She looks in bad shape."

"She is, George. Some bush-whackin' pole-cat shot her!" Dusty said with mounting anger.

"I don't know if I can do much for her, Dusty. I'm not a doctor."

"I know, George, but you're the closest thing we've got to one. You've got ta try."

Just as George started to speak, the bell over the front door jingled and one of the miners from up on Palmer Creek stepped in, and seeing the crisis, rushed to help. "Step aside," he said with a voice of authority and started ordering stuff off the shelf behind the counter where George kept first-aid supplies. "Get me plenty of hot water and clean bandages. This animal has lost a lot of blood, and if we don't stop the bleeding, I'm afraid she's a goner."

After cleaning the wound, the miner asked for and received a needle and a length of sinew to stitch up the bullet hole. Through all this, Shadow Spirit didn't move or make a sound. Her eyes were open and watchful, but somehow, she knew that the stranger was there to help.

Afterward, he apologized for his bluntness and said that he was sorry he could do no more for, as he put it, "this magnificent creature." He said they would have to watch her close for fever and to keep her as still as possible. If she could make it through the night, she had a good chance of surviving.

"Thanks for everything you've done, Mr. ...uh?"

"Folks call me Doc, Doc Jones," the stranger said with a pleasant smile. "I was glad I happened into town and could help."

"Well, my name's Dusty, and if I can ever return the kindness, ya be sure and ask."

"We're sure glad you're here 'bouts. This town's needed a doc for a mighty long time," George said with excitement in his voice.

"Wait a second, wait a second. I said they call me Doc. I didn't say I was a doctor. I came north looking for gold, just like everyone else. I'm not a doctor anymore."

Even though he said it with conviction, Dusty could see sadness in his eyes that wasn't there before.

"Hey! You're not by any chance the feller that operated on ol' Dynamite Johnny down in Homer, are ya?"

"Yes, yes I am. I had no choice. He would have surely died if I hadn't."

"If you're not a doctor, you sure did a good imitation of one. Johnny's up and about and as mean as ever. He said you saved his life!"

George didn't want to press Doc Jones about his past, but the town needed a doctor, and the storekeeper wasn't going to let this prospect get away if he could help it.

"Dynamite Johnny said you used to be a doctor. What made you quit?"

"I don't think that's any of your business," he said curtly, turning his attention back to Shadow Spirit, dismissing the subject.

George, realizing it was futile to pursue the subject any further, busied himself about the store.

After checking his handy work one more time, Doc Jones said he would return in the morning and look in on her if she was still alive.

The kindhearted storekeeper brought out a box and a blanket from the back room. He made a comfortable bed for Shadow Spirit by the potbellied stove, and together, he and Dusty moved the injured wolf-dog into the comfortable bed.

That night, Dusty didn't leave Shadow Spirit's side. Aura Lee brought him food and sat by the fire part of the night to share the grief with her husband. At times, the great animal would whimper in pain, but never did she try to rise. Dusty would gently stroke her head and soothe her with soft words of encouragement, feeling the pain of his faithful companion.

Sometime in the night, Aura Lee slipped off to bed and Dusty dozed, dreaming sporadically of the past adventures he and Shadow Spirit had shared.

Long about daybreak, he was startled by something warm and wet crossing his cheeks. Opening his eyes, his heart leaped into his throat, for standing over him, looking down with those piercing green eyes, was Shadow Spirit.

"Easy girl, ya shouldn't be up movin' around. Come on. Let's get ya back in your box." Dusty carefully picked up the weak wolf-dog and took her back to her bed, saying, "Ya best stay right here fer a while and rest, and later on taday, I'll fetch ya home."

Shadow Spirit, seeming to understand what Dusty said to her, put her head on her paws and closed her eyes.

Later, over breakfast with Aura Lee and his friends, George and Mrs. Roll, Dusty spoke of his surprise awaking. They found it hard to believe that just yesterday, Shadow Spirit was at death's door and already she was up on her feet. They all agreed that she had extraordinary healing powers, but nothing ever surprised Dusty when it came to Shadow Spirit's capabilities.

After breakfast, Dusty told Aura Lee that this business of being shot at and all the other things happening around Hope had to come to a stop, and it had to stop now.

Aura Lee knew what her husband meant, and she could see the determination in his eyes.

"Do be careful, and don't take any chances, and… and—"

Aura Lee didn't have a chance to finish before Dusty swept her up in his arms, kissed her tenderly, and said, "I'll be fine, darlin'. Don't you worry yer pretty little head about that!" With that said he turned her loose and headed for the door. As he opened it, he turned and, with a boyish grin on his face, asked, "Hey, have I told ya lately that you're 'bout as pretty as a new speckled puppy!" With that, he turned back and was gone, leaving Aura Lee remembering the first time he said that to her. It seemed so long ago.

CHAPTER 37

After seeing the wolf-dog fall, Jake continued to fire his rifle until it was empty. *Who knows?* He thought to himself. *I might get lucky and hit that fool lawman too.* Not knowing whether he had or hadn't, he had no desire to stick around and find out, so before the echo of the last shot died, he slipped into the deep forest and headed back to his hideout.

As Jake approached his camp, he stopped before entering the clearing. He didn't need any surprises at this juncture of his plans. He stayed hidden for a good ten minutes before he walked up to the man that was gagged and tied lying next to the fire. Jake gave the defenseless man a swift kick, catching the semi-conscious gambler a wicked blow in his unprotected ribs.

"Wake up, Champbell!" Jake yelled, kicking at the helpless man.

"Please," Johnny pleaded in a barely audible voice. "Please…I-I need water."

"Shut up. You'll have plenty of water when I get rid of ya over yonder in that inlet. If ya hadn't a recognized me when I came into Scotty's, you'd still be fleecin' them miners of their hard-earned gold instead of fixin' ta be fish food. When ya think about it, ya ain't any different than me except ya cheat them out of their gold with a deck of cards and I just flat-out steal it from 'em." Thinking himself funny, he broke out laughing at his own remarks. Ignoring his captive, he turned his back on the suffering gambler and commenced preparing a cold meal for himself.

He wouldn't have time to eat later if he was going to sneak into the mining camp he discovered a few days ago upon that little no-name stream near Six-Mile Creek. *The old fool running it thought no one would discover his digs in that hidden valley, but I guess he didn't count on old Jake a-sniffin' it out,* he thought to himself.

Jake had lain for two days, hidden in the brush near the old prospector's claim, watching his routine. He knew the old coot headed back to his cabin up at the far end of the valley about an hour before dark. He also knew that the old-timer stashed his gold under a big rock near the stream.

At first, Jake thought this rather strange, but then, the more he thought about it, the more he realized the old prospector was smarter than he looked. If anyone found his cabin and tried to steal his gold, they would come up empty. And unless they saw where he buried it at night by the mine, they could spend weeks searching his camp and still not find anything. By waiting until the miner left, it would be as easy as taking candy from a baby, not like that first claim he had jumped. There he was almost caught when the prospector came up on him while he was rifling through his tent. It was a piece of luck that he had heard him coming and was able to lay the miner out with the barrel of his six-gun.

Jake had always been a petty criminal from his teen years until now and never earned an honest dollar. He had been in and out of the calaboose several times for insignificant amounts of time. That is, until he robbed a Wells Fargo stage down in Arizona Territory and was tracked down by a US marshal and convicted of a federal crime. He had robbed stages before without causing so much grief for himself. What he didn't realize at the time of the hold-up was one of the passengers was a US senator, and the gold he had stolen belonged to the government.

The marshal relentlessly dogged him for months, finally catching him in a little mining camp in Colorado. The lawman then took him back East for trial, which was short and quick, putting him in federal prison in a place called Leavenworth, Kansas. He was sentenced to ten years at hard labor, and he vowed that when he got out, he'd kill the marshal who put him there.

As Jake lay in his tent, wondering how much gold the old miner had hidden, his mind kept going back to the burning hate he had for that US marshal who had put him in a stinking prison. He couldn't believe his luck. Who would ever have thought he was going to be rich when he got through with these mindless fools, and at the same time, was going to be able to exact a torturous revenge on the man responsible for his ten long years in prison? He didn't care what the man called himself up here in this desolate land. He would have recognized him anywhere, with or without a beard.

"Well, Dusty Sourdough, or whatever you call yourself, you're a dead man. I knew I'd find ya sooner or later. Yep! The end of the road has come for the famous marshal…"

Jake froze in mid-sentence as the shadow of a man loomed over him with a rifle in his hand, his rifle, and the man, to Jake's total astonishment, was none other than Johnny Champbell. Jake saw the hate in the gambler's eyes and knew if he didn't make a move, he'd be bear bait.

Stalling for time, Jake asked in a trembling voice, "H-How'd ya get loose? I should've finished ya when I had the chance."

"Shut up!" Johnny shrieked in a voice that he himself didn't recognize. "You're done stealin' around here. We ain't got any law here 'bouts, so I'm your judge 'n jury."

"Ya can't just shoot me," Jake pleaded. "What about yer marshal? Take me to him!" By now, Jake could see that Johnny was very weak from lack of food and the treatment he had handed out. It was all the gambler could do to hold the rifle and stand. Jake could see his hands trembling and knew he was about to collapse. All Jake had to do was keep him talking.

"Marshal? What marshal? We don't have—"Johnny's head began to spin, and he could barely make the words he wanted to say come out.

Johnny could see Jake's lips moving, but his voice sounded funny and far away. It was as if he was talking from inside a tunnel, and the words were distorted. Then he saw that Jake was starting to stand and come toward him, but the rifle was too heavy to bring to bear on him. And then a shot rang out, and he was falling.

CHAPTER 38

Dusty headed for the spot where he and Shadow Spirit were bushwhacked the day before. With any luck, whoever did the shooting would have left some sign. Carefully combing the area, Dusty picked up the tracks of the dry gulcher.

"Well, well," he said to himself. "Looks like the same owl hoot that's been sneaking around here 'bouts. Well, Jake or whoever ya are, it's time to pay up fer terrorizing my wife and shootin' my wolf-dog." Dusty looked in the direction the tracks headed, checked his rifle, and started after them.

The day seemed never ending as Dusty followed the tracks he found earlier that day where he and Shadow Spirit had been attacked. She had wanted to come with him, and her recuperative powers were remarkable, but Dusty knew she wasn't well enough to travel. Now, as he rested and chewed on a piece of jerked moose, he was missing his companion. He sat there, pondering the strange events that had been going on around Hope. The claim jumping's, the disappearance of Johnny Champbell over in Sunrise, Aura Lee being watched, and now Shadow Spirit taking lead; somehow, they all tied together.

After finishing his meager lunch, Dusty got back to the business at hand. The trail led into a blind canyon off Bear Creek. As far as Dusty knew, no one lived or worked a claim in the canyon. A few prospectors had struck color down on the lower part of Bear Creek, but the ones who had tried it up this way had come up dry. The only one who was taking out any gold along the creek worth talking about was Curley. *Wait a minute!* Didn't George tell him Curley was the first one to be robbed?

Well now, Dusty thought. *Things are startin' ta come together.*

As Dusty entered into the rugged canyon, he could see why prospecting would be practically impossible. On one side, the walls went straight up, and there wasn't any evidence of water anywhere to be seen. The trail he was following was rugged and faint at best. It wound around large boulders and was pretty much overgrown with alder brush. Several times, he lost the trail and had to backtrack 'til he found where he went wrong.

It was one of these times when Dusty had lost the trail backtracking. He discovered where his quarry had veered off the faint game trail and headed toward a thick stand of timber to the right. In every direction, the alder brush blocked his path. Dropping to his knees, Dusty started searching the ground for any clue that would suggest the direction the owl hoot was traveling. After a moment or two of looking on all fours, he determined by an almost-invisible heel print that the culprit was headed straight for the stand of timber. Dusty found the farther he worked his way in the direction of the spruce trees, the density of the alder brush became less and less. Once or twice, he spotted a scuff mark indicating that he was headed in the right direction.

Scratched and bleeding from the wild rose bushes that seemed to thrive in amongst the alder brush, Dusty was happy to come upon a small clearing, where he decided to stop and pull some of the small, irritating stickers out of his buckskins. Finding an outcrop of rocks that rose above the surrounding brush, he decided to climb to the top and have a look-see before resting a spell.

As he started to ascend the jagged outcrop, a shot rang out. With catlike reflexes, Dusty leaped to the ground and took cover behind the rocks. The shot had come from the woods he was headed for. After waiting for a few moments, no other shots were fired, so he poked his head out from the rock he had ducked behind. Carefully, he stood up, and when nothing happened, he moved off into the brush a few paces in the direction the shot had come from and waited.

Had Jake spotted him? Was he now the hunted instead of the hunter? As these questions went through Dusty's mind, his ears were tuned to his surroundings. He was aware of the slightest movements, and when the sound of nature returned to normal, he moved out like a shadow, leaving nothing to indicate his passing.

Slipping into the trees, Dusty stopped to listen to the sounds of the forest. Satisfied that he was alone, he scouted around until he picked up the trail he had been following. After a short distance, the dense trees began to thin out. The brush was nearly nonexistent, and the trail was clear and easy to follow. Stopping again to listen to the sounds around him, he was assured, as best he could be without Shadow Spirit by his side to warn him, that he was very much alone.

Up ahead, he could see where the forest opened into a clearing. Dusty figured that somewhere close was where the shot had to have come from. Not wanting to take any chances, he circled around the clearing and approached it from the opposite side. There was a slight breeze moving the leaves and ruffling his beard, and this he knew was in his favor. Sound as well as smell carries on the wind, and before Dusty was in sight of the clearing, he heard voices. Ducking down low, he moved cautiously ahead until he could see two men.

One was standing over the other with a rifle. The man lying on the ground looked to be in bad shape. His face was battered and bruised. From where Dusty was, he could tell that the poor fellow's voice was weak and most of his strength was gone. As he watched the dramas unfold before him, Dusty saw the man with the rifle lever a round into the chamber.

Dusty sprung from his place of concealment, shouting and levering his own Winchester, firing as rapidly as possible. He wasn't really trying to hit the man with the rifle. He was too close to the man on the ground, so he fired above the polecat's head.

Caught totally by surprise, Jake spun around and fired at the same time. This caused his first shot to go wide, crashing into a spruce tree to the left of the on-charging Dusty. Jake's second shot came much closer.

It sounded like a mad hornet as it passed within inches of Dusty's ear. Diving and rolling as he hit the ground, Dusty hoped he could get a clear shot. As he came up on one knee to fire back, he saw Jake dart for the trees beyond his camp. Dusty snapped off a quick shot but saw it miss as it took out a chunk of tree bark near the retreating Jake. Before he could lever another round into his rifle, Jake disappeared into the deep forest.

Dusty ran to the man lying motionless on the ground. At first, he feared that a stray bullet might have hit him. Dropping to his knees, he felt for a pulse. After a moment, he was relieved to find one, however faint it was. At least he was still alive. At first, Dusty barely recognized him to be Johnny Champbell, the missing gambler from Sunrise. Looking about, Dusty spotted a canteen lying near the tent. Retrieving it, he raised Johnny's head and poured a few drops on his lips. Johnny's eyes fluttered opened and stared up into Dusty's face, at first with fear, but as recognition came to the gambler's clouded mind, the fear changed to relief.

"I…I thought I was a goner," the grateful gambler tried to say in a weak voice.

"Don't try to talk right now," Dusty said with compassion. "I'll try an patch ya up as best I can, and then I'll get ya back ta town fer some proper fixin'. We've got a real doc, and he's a right good one too!"

After boiling water and cleaning Johnny's wounds, Dusty was thankful the shot he had heard earlier hadn't hit the gambler. After making Johnny as comfortable as he could, Dusty went about making a hot broth with some of the moose jerky he had in his possible bag and wild herbs growing in abundance in the forest. It wasn't the tastiest meal the gambler would ever have, but it was hot and nourishing.

The food revived Johnny somewhat, so he began to tell of his ordeal that had almost ended his life. As the story unfolded, Dusty started to put the pieces together.

This Jake was a bad one, rotten through and through, and as Johnny rambled on, Dusty's thoughts drifted back to the Old West and his marshaling days.

He now knew why the stranger he had run into in George Roll's store looked familiar. A life time ago, he had tracked this outlaw all over the Southwest and up into Colorado before he finally caught up to him and sent him to federal prison. When Dusty turned him over to another US marshal for the train ride back to Leavenworth, the last words the criminal spit at Dusty was, "When I get out, I'm gonna find ya, and then yer gonna pay!"

Dusty's thoughts were interrupted by the sound of Johnny's snoring. He was so caught up in his thoughts of the past that he hadn't even noticed when the gambler had drifted off to sleep.

At first light, Dusty threw more wood on the fire that he had kept burning all night. Not knowing whether Jake would try to dry gulch them in their sleep, Dusty had decided to keep watch all night.

"Good morning!" Johnny said with a cheery and much stronger voice. "That coffee sure smells good," he said as he struggled to stand.

Dusty could see that the man was still in pain, but he had to admire him because not a word of complaint came from his lips.

After a meager breakfast, with Johnny's help, Dusty searched Jake's hideout for any clues. It wasn't long before things that had been going on around Hope started to make sense. They found empty pokes with different miners' initials on them, along with other belongings that had been reported stolen.

"Well, I reckon we found the pole-cat that's been robbin' all the miners here 'bouts!" Dusty exclaimed. "We'll get ya ta town, and then I'll go huntin' me a lowdown critter. We don't need his kind around here!"

Even though Johnny was weak from his ordeal, the pair made good time returning to Hope. It was past noon when they walked into George Roll's store. After telling George what they had found out, Dusty said he was going after the no-good thief and bring him back for trial.

"Now how in tarnation are ya gonna do that?" George asked with a bewildered look. "We don't have any law here 'bouts, and the only judge is up in Nome."

"We can send word fer the judge ta come down here. As fer as not havin' any law, I'll handle that!"

Dusty didn't give George time to reply or ask any more questions. He abruptly did an about-face and headed out the door, leaving the storekeeper and Johnny with puzzled looks on their faces.

⌒

When Dusty didn't return home the same day he had left, Aura Lee elected to leave the hospitality and safety of the Rolls' for the familiar surroundings of her own home. With Shadow Spirit well on the road to recovery, she felt safe, knowing that the great wolf-dog would protect her.

⌒

The smoke curling from the little cabin's chimney told Dusty that his Aura Lee was at her stove, humming to herself as she cooked a tasty meal for her husband. This gave Dusty a warm feeling inside, a feeling that he never knew existed until Aura Lee came into his life.

"Howdy in the cabin!" Dusty shouted, proclaiming his arrival so as not to startle Aura Lee by just barging in the door.

The door burst open, and first out was Shadow Spirit. In one bounding leap, she cleared the porch steps and, in an instant, had her front paws in the middle of Dusty's chest, giving him a "right proper face washing."

"Hey, it's my turn!" Aura Lee shouted with glee as she ran to Dusty and threw her arms around him.

What a homecoming. It was as if he had been gone for weeks when, in reality, it had only been a couple of days.

Dusty waited until after dinner to tell Aura Lee that he was leaving again in the morning to track down Jake.

⌒

Sitting by the big, rock fireplace with its cheerful fire burning brightly, they related to each other all that had happened since they had parted. When all was said, they just held each other's hand and soaked in the comfort of the love they felt for each other. The moment was broken by the growl that came from deep within Shadow Spirit's chest. In one swift movement, Dusty was at the door with his Colt in hand and Shadow Spirit by his side.

"Easy, girl," he spoke softly as he thumbed back the hammer of his six-gun. "You stay," he commanded the wolf-dog, and at the same time, he slipped back the latch on the heavy plank door. Turning his head slightly, he said to Aura Lee in a low voice, bar the door behind me." And then, like a shadow, he was gone.

It wasn't quite dark yet, even though the hour was late. Dusty moved to the corner of the cabin without a sound and stood in the dark like a statue. The only detectable movement he made was his eyes scanning the surrounding forest. Nothing seemed out of place, and Dusty started to go back inside when, all at once, a blood-curdling scream shattered the stillness.

Dusty charged headlong into the trees. He didn't know what he might find. By the sound of it, someone was getting a hurt put on them pretty bad. As he got closer to the fracas, he started yelling at the top of his lungs, hoping the sound of his voice would scare off whatever it was that was doing the damage.

The first thing Dusty saw was the fleeting shadow of a man heading away from him. It was obvious that the small clearing he was standing in was where the battle had taken place. Alder brush was broken down all around, and there were traces of blood on the ground. After further inspection, Dusty found human as well as animal tracks.

"Well I'll be," Dusty exclaimed, "these here tracks look like they belong to that doggone cat! Whoever Dog got a piece of sure didn't want me ta find him, and I can just 'bout guess who that person is."

Dusty decided against following whom he believed was Jake. In the morning would be soon enough. Then he would start the hunt for this outlaw in earnest.

Returning to the cabin, Dusty found Aura Lee clutching his Winchester and trembling with fear. After calming her jangled nerves, he told her what had alerted Shadow Spirit. After Dusty assured her that the danger had passed, Aura Lee told Dusty of how Dog seemed to know Shadow Spirit was hurt and not up to par. The fierce little cat, on her own, had taken over the job of protector of her new family, and boy did Jake find out the hard way.

CHAPTER 39

Jake was beginning to think he was jinxed. The only lucky thing that happened to him was that fool gambler passing out when he did. If he would have lasted another minute, he would have drilled him dead center with that rifle.

He lay with his face in a stream, trying to take some of the sting out of the scratches he had received from the lynx that jumped him from out of nowhere. He was sure that the only luck he had was bad. To top it all off, he had Dusty in his sights when that fool cat had jumped him. However, he thought to himself, he did have a little luck on his side. He had managed to get away from that screaming, clawing cat before Dusty got to him in the woods.

The wounds were numerous and deep, and Jake was still bleeding when he left the creek and headed for his new camp. Tomorrow would be different, he thought to himself; tomorrow, he would steal the gold from that old fool he had been watching up on the river. After that, he would lie in wait for Dusty and gun him down the moment he came into sight.

Dusty was first up in the morning. He wanted to get an early start and end all this claim-jumping and ambushing once and for all. Reaching under the bed, Dusty pulled out a pair of old saddlebags. He hadn't opened them or even given them any thought since arriving in Alaska. He carried them downstairs and tossed them on the kitchen table and then turned to the chore of making morning coffee.

"Good morning!" a sweet, cheerful voice said from the kitchen doorway. "You're up awful early." Aura Lee crossed the kitchen and kissed him on the cheek. Turning, she noticed the saddlebags lying on the table. "What are those old dirty saddlebags laying on my clean table for? I thought you had thrown those filthy things away."

"No," Dusty said with a touch of sadness in his voice. "No. I kept them, hoping I would never have ta use what I put away inside them."

Walking over to the table, he unbuckled the worn leather flap of the saddlebag and reached inside. He pulled out a small, highly polished rosewood box and what looked to be a very official-looking document. Dusty stood for a moment, staring at the little box, and then spoke with regret in his voice as he opened it.

"I never thought, after moving up here, I would ever pin this here badge back on. When I tried ta resign, they wouldn't let me. Instead, they issued that there warrant," he said, pointing at the document he had laid on the table. "It commissions me as a United States Marshal at large. Now that Alaska has become a US territory this past year, I guess it means I am legally obliged ta uphold the law. I never wanted ta pin this on again," he said as he fastened it to his shirt. "But someone has ta stop Jake and stop him now!"

All of a sudden, the sound of a scuffle broke out on the porch, ending the conversation and the uncomfortable moment between them. Bounding to door, Dusty jerked it open with one hand, and in that same instant, he filled the other with his Colt. Looking toward the end of the porch, where the commotion was coming from, Dusty broke into uncontrollable laughter.

"Hey, you two!" he shouted, trying to get his laughter under control. "Lighten up on that there poor ol' wolf-dog," he laughingly said to Dog, who looked to be getting the better of his best friend, Shadow Spirit.

Dusty was more than happy to see Shadow Spirit almost fully recovered. He decided that she was well enough to hit the trail after Jake. He knew she could find him much quicker than he could, and besides, he really felt lost without her by his side.

Getting his gear together and saying good-bye to Aura Lee, Dusty and Shadow Spirit headed out the door and up the trail to whatever destiny awaited them. The morning was cool, and clouds covered the sky in a solid mass of gray. Dusty hoped the rain would hold off a day or two more, but by the looks of the low-hanging clouds, that wasn't about to happen.

It wasn't hard to pick up the trail from where the scuffle had taken place in the woods the night before. Dog had done enough damage to Jake that the trail was marked every few feet with generous drops of blood.

By noon, a few drops of rain had begun to fall. The trail had been easy to follow thus far, and Dusty was less apprehensive about the rain washing out any sign. Dusty knew Jake was moving as fast as he could and wasn't even trying to cover his tracks. Stopping beside a small stream for a rest, Dusty could tell that Shadow Spirit had no desire to slow down, so after a cool drink, they kept moving ahead.

As the day wore on, the rain worsened and was now a full blown storm. For the past five miles or so, Dusty had relied on Shadow Spirit's ability to track. This didn't worry him. He knew there wasn't much of a chance of Jake giving the great wolf-dog the slip, rainstorm or not.

When Jake had finally made it to his makeshift camp, the gravity of his run-in with the lynx was apparent. Until this point, the fear of being caught was a strong driving force, and now that he felt somewhat safe in his own camp, the pain and the weakness from the loss of blood were starting to take effect. After a close inspection of the deeper cuts the cat had inflicted, Jake, being trail-wise, knew enough to know that he had to clean the wounds with hot water and then bandage them tightly to stop the slow but steady loss of blood.

It was hard to get a fire going in the steady downpour, but after two or three tries, the flames took off, and soon, Jake had water boiling and even a pot of coffee on.

He was thankful that he had bolstered up enough nerve to return to his old camp after Dusty and that fool gambler had left. At least now, he had his essentials and he could make plans for his next move.

After he doctored himself and gulped down a couple cups of hot coffee, Jake felt better and wanted to lie down and sleep, but he knew he couldn't. When the rain stopped, he had no doubt that Dusty, if not the whole town, would be on his trail with hanging on their mind. He had to scout around and find an escape route heading out of this desolate country before they caught up to him.

He knew he wasn't far from the inlet, so he decided that he would head in that direction and, with any luck, he might find a boat one of the natives left on shore. Jake gathered up what little he could carry on his back, figuring he could steal whatever else he needed along the way. For all the stealing and treachery he had committed around Hope, the only thing he had to show for it, besides his wounds, was one small poke of gold he had stolen and had been carrying in his pocket all this time.

❧

Dusty knew that his quarry was near. The smell of wood smoke in the air and the excitement Shadow Spirit showed was enough warning to call her to his side and move ahead with caution. The first warning Dusty had that the camp was near came in the form of a low growl from Shadow Spirit. Not wanting to approach the camp head on, he and Shadow Spirit circled around and came up on it from the opposite direction. The rain had slowed some, but it was still coming down hard enough to hide any noise Dusty made as he cautiously approached the camp.

Dusty watched the camp from his place of concealment for a short time and then realized that something was obviously wrong about it. He boldly got to his feet and walked up to the warm, burning fire. A quick glance around the camp told Dusty that Jake had left in a hurry, only taking the bare essentials he could carry on his back.

"He hasn't been gone long, girl. Go find him. Show me which way he went. We got 'im now!"

The trail heading down to the inlet was steep and, because of the rain, very slick. Jake fell several times getting to the bottom and was unrecognizable when he reached it. He was covered with mud from head to foot. By now, he was almost in a panicked state of mind, and his appearance was the least of his worries. He had been on the wrong side of the law for so many years that he had developed a sixth sense of knowing when they were closing in on him, and he had that uncomfortable feeling right now.

Reaching the inlet, Jake looked first right and then left, hoping to spot a boat he could steal. Not seeing one, he started off to his left, moving as fast as he could. When he was about to give up and head back inland, he came upon a small cove, and on its shore were several canoes. *At last,* he thought, *my luck has changed.* Why all those boats were on shore and not out on the water with their native owners, doing their daily fishing, crossed his mind quickly as he headed toward them.

The other strange thing he noticed was how far away the natives were from their boats, and he also wondered why the ropes tying the canoes reached a good two hundred yards inland. Seeing the natives so far from their canoes he considered to be more good luck, and the long lines, well, his knife would make short order of that problem.

Bursting onto the beach at a full run, Jake was not noticed by the natives until he was cutting the rope of the first canoe he came to. He looked up and saw that he had been spotted. The natives were on the high ground next to their fire, jumping up and down and frantically waving at him, but to his total amazement, none were charging down to the beach in pursuit of him and their stolen canoe. Again, not trying to figure out what seemed to be more good luck, Jake paddled farther out into the inlet and didn't stop until he was sure he was beyond the reach of any pursuit.

He was near total exhaustion when he laid the paddle down to rest. What he saw when he looked toward the beach made him shout with joy. He couldn't believe his eyes. The natives had caught his pursuer and were dragging him, kicking and hollering, back up to their fire.

"Well, at last," Jake said out loud. "It ain't exactly what I had in mind fer that mettlin' marshal, but I reckon natives will make short work of Dusty."

Hearing a low rumble that seemed to be getting closer with each passing moment, Jake turned to see, with horror-stricken eyes, a wall of water twenty feet high coming at him like a runaway freight train. Panic filled his mind, and his last thought, his very last thought as this mountain of water came crashing

down and crushed the life from him, was, *Dusty lives…*
they were…

CHAPTER 40

Dog was leisurely stretched out on the porch as if he owned the place when Dusty and Shadow Spirit came up the trail. Dusty was still amazed how that cat had adopted them and was now a part of the family. As he stepped onto the porch, he ruffled the soft fur on the ornery little cat's neck, and Dog turned playfully on his back and lazily swatted at Dusty.

"Hey ya, fur ball," Dusty said affectionately as he attempted to rub the cat's belly. "I fergot ta thank ya fer the other night. I reckon if it weren't fer ya, I'd a takin' some lead. I'm much obliged!" Giving Dog a loving pat on the head, he stepped on in the cabin and into Aura Lee's loving arms.

"Is…is it over?" she asked with a tremble in her voice.

"Yep, sweetheart, it's over," he said as he held her tightly in his arms. "He won't be a-botherin' us or anybody else anymore." Then he explained all the events that took place up to where the Athabascans had saved his life.

"Why, I thought them natives figured I was a-fixin' ta steal another one of their boats like Jake did, and they were a-stoppin' me, but that weren't it at all. They was a-savin' my hide! They pulled me up ta high ground just as the cannonball of a bore tide came roaring through. Jake didn't stand a chance. He was a goner."

Dusty then reached into his pocket and pulled out his marshals' badge and said, "I didn't need this after all. I guess we can keep my secret around here a while longer."

With that said, he got the polished wooden box he had taken it from, returned it to its place, and closed the lid.

Aura Lee and Dusty spent the rest of the day catching each other up on all the events that had taken place.

"Oh yeah," Dusty said with a twinkle in his eye, "I almost fergot." He walked over to his possible bag hanging on a peg by the plank door and pulled something out.

He told Aura Lee to close her eyes and hold out her hand. When she did, he dropped the object he had fished out of his possible bag into her hand.

She gasped when her eyes opened and fell on the heavy little object in her hand. "It's gold!" she shouted with glee. "I've never seen anything like it! Where did it come from? Is there more? Can we—?"

Dusty interrupted her barrage of questions. "Honey, I don't know if there's any more like that one, but look at this." He then dumped the rest of his possible bag on the table and showed Aura Lee the gold that had collected in it. "I do know there's more where this came from, but I can't figure out how ta get at it. Ya know when I was trapped in that underground cavern I told ya about? That gold had ta come from there. That was the only time I was in the water. If I could find another way in ta that cavern, we'd be set fer life. Who knows? Maybe there is another way in, and maybe one day, with some luck, I just might find it."

At last peace came to Dusty and Aura Lee and calm fell over the little communities of Hope and Sunrise. Things returned to normal as everyone prepared for the long, cold winter ahead.

listen|imagine|view|experience

AUDIO BOOK DOWNLOAD INCLUDED WITH THIS BOOK!

In your hands you hold a complete digital entertainment package. In addition to the paper version, you receive a free download of the audio version of this book. Simply use the code listed below when visiting our website. Once downloaded to your computer, you can listen to the book through your computer's speakers, burn it to an audio CD or save the file to your portable music device (such as Apple's popular iPod) and listen on the go!

How to get your free audio book digital download:

1. Visit www.tatepublishing.com and click on the e|LIVE logo on the home page.
2. Enter the following coupon code:
   33c9-4400-5f68-0a4e-fb1d-c5c5-a0f1-e6593.
   Download the audio book from your e|LIVE digital locker and begin enjoying your new digital entertainment package today!